THE PELICAN SHAKESPEARE

GENERAL EDITOR ALFRED HARBAGE

CORIOLANUS

WILLIAM SHAKESPEARE

CORIOLANUS

EDITED BY HARRY LEVIN

PENGUIN BOOKS

Penguin Books
625 Madison Avenue
New York, New York 10022

First published in *The Pelican Shakespeare* 1956
This revised edition first published 1973
Reprinted 1975, 1978

Library of Congress catalog card number: 70-98376

Printed in the United States of America by
Kingsport Press, Inc., Kingsport, Tennessee
Set in Monotype Ehrhardt

CONTENTS

Shakespeare and his Stage   7

The Texts of the Plays   12

Introduction   14

Note on the Text   23

Coriolanus   25

PUBLISHER'S NOTE

Soon after the thirty-eight volumes forming *The Pelican Shakespeare* had been published, they were brought together in *The Complete Pelican Shakespeare*. The editorial revisions and new textual features are explained in detail in the General Editor's Preface to the one-volume edition. They have all been incorporated in the present volume. The following should be mentioned in particular:

The lines are not numbered in arbitrary units. Instead all lines are numbered which contain a word, phrase, or allusion explained in the glossarial notes. In the occasional instances where there is a long stretch of unannotated text, certain lines are numbered in italics to serve the conventional reference purpose.

The intrusive and often inaccurate place-headings inserted by early editors are omitted (as is becoming standard practise), but for the convenience of those who miss them, an indication of locale now appears as first item in the annotation of each scene.

In the interest of both elegance and utility, each speech-prefix is set in a separate line when the speaker's lines are in verse, except when these words form the second half of a pentameter line. Thus the verse form of the speech is kept visually intact, and turned-over lines are avoided. What is printed as verse and what is printed as prose has, in general, the authority of the original texts. Departures from the original texts in this regard have only the authority of editorial tradition and the judgment of the Pelican editors; and, in a few instances, are admittedly arbitrary.

SHAKESPEARE AND
HIS STAGE

William Shakespeare was christened in Holy Trinity
Church, Stratford-upon-Avon, April 26, 1564. His birth
is traditionally assigned to April 23. He was the eldest of
four boys and two girls who survived infancy in the family
of John Shakespeare, glover and trader of Henley Street,
and his wife Mary Arden, daughter of a small landowner
of Wilmcote. In 1568 John was elected Bailiff (equivalent
to Mayor) of Stratford, having already filled the minor
municipal offices. The town maintained for the sons of the
burgesses a free school, taught by a university graduate
and offering preparation in Latin sufficient for university
entrance; its early registers are lost, but there can be little
doubt that Shakespeare received the formal part of his
education in this school.

On November 27, 1582, a license was issued for the
marriage of William Shakespeare (aged eighteen) and Ann
Hathaway (aged twenty-six), and on May 26, 1583, their
child Susanna was christened in Holy Trinity Church.
The inference that the marriage was forced upon the youth
is natural but not inevitable; betrothal was legally binding
at the time, and was sometimes regarded as conferring
conjugal rights. Two additional children of the marriage,
the twins Hamnet and Judith, were christened on Feb-
ruary 2, 1585. Meanwhile the prosperity of the elder
Shakespeares had declined, and William was impelled to
seek a career outside Stratford.

The tradition that he spent some time as a country

teacher is old but unverifiable. Because of the absence of records his early twenties are called the "lost years," and only one thing about them is certain – that at least some of these years were spent in winning a place in the acting profession. He may have begun as a provincial trouper, but by 1592 he was established in London and prominent enough to be attacked. In a pamphlet of that year, *Groats-worth of Wit*, the ailing Robert Greene complained of the neglect which university writers like himself had suffered from actors, one of whom was daring to set up as a playwright:

. . . an vpstart Crow, beautified with our feathers, that with his *Tygers hart wrapt in a Players hyde*, supposes he is as well able to bombast out a blanke verse as the best of you: and beeing an absolute *Iohannes fac totum*, is in his owne conceit the onely Shake-scene in a countrey.

The pun on his name, and the parody of his line "O tiger's heart wrapped in a woman's hide" (*3 Henry VI*), pointed clearly to Shakespeare. Some of his admirers protested, and Henry Chettle, the editor of Greene's pamphlet, saw fit to apologize:

. . . I am as sory as if the originall fault had beene my fault, because my selfe haue seene his demeanor no lesse ciuill than he excelent in the qualitie he professes: Besides, diuers of worship haue reported his vprightnes of dealing, which argues his honesty, and his facetious grace in writting, that approoues his Art. (Prefatory epistle, *Kind-Harts Dreame*)

The plague closed the London theatres for many months in 1592–94, denying the actors their livelihood. To this period belong Shakespeare's two narrative poems, *Venus and Adonis* and *The Rape of Lucrece*, both dedicated to the Earl of Southampton. No doubt the poet was rewarded with a gift of money as usual in such cases, but he did no further dedicating and we have no reliable information on whether Southampton, or anyone else, became his regular patron. His sonnets, first mentioned in 1598 and published without his consent in 1609, are intimate without being

explicitly autobiographical. They seem to commemorate
the poet's friendship with an idealized youth, rivalry with
a more favored poet, and love affair with a dark mistress;
and his bitterness when the mistress betrays him in con-
junction with the friend; but it is difficult to decide pre-
cisely what the "story" is, impossible to decide whether it
is fictional or true. The true distinction of the sonnets, at
least of those not purely conventional, rests in the uni-
versality of the thoughts and moods they express, and in
their poignancy and beauty.

In 1594 was formed the theatrical company known until
1603 as the Lord Chamberlain's men, thereafter as the
King's men. Its original membership included, besides
Shakespeare, the beloved clown Will Kempe and the
famous actor Richard Burbage. The company acted in
various London theatres and even toured the provinces,
but it is chiefly associated in our minds with the Globe
Theatre built on the south bank of the Thames in 1599.
Shakespeare was an actor and joint owner of this company
(and its Globe) through the remainder of his creative
years. His plays, written at the average rate of two a year,
together with Burbage's acting won it its place of leadership among the London companies.

Individual plays began to appear in print, in editions
both honest and piratical, and the publishers became in-
creasingly aware of the value of Shakespeare's name on
the title pages. As early as 1598 he was hailed as the leading
English dramatist in the *Palladis Tamia* of Francis
Meres:

As *Plautus* and *Seneca* are accounted the best for Comedy and
Tragedy among the Latines, so *Shakespeare* among the English is
the most excellent in both kinds for the stage: for Comedy, witnes
his *Gentlemen of Verona*, his *Errors*, his *Loue labors lost*, his *Loue
labours wonne* [at one time in print but no longer extant, at least
under this title], his *Midsummers night dream*, & his *Merchant of
Venice*; for Tragedy, his *Richard the 2*, *Richard the 3*, *Henry the 4*,
King Iohn, *Titus Andronicus*, and his *Romeo and Iuliet*.

The note is valuable both in indicating Shakespeare's prestige and in helping us to establish a chronology. In the second half of his writing career, history plays gave place to the great tragedies; and farces and light comedies gave place to the problem plays and symbolic romances. In 1623, seven years after his death, his former fellow-actors, John Heminge and Henry Condell, cooperated with a group of London printers in bringing out his plays in collected form. The volume is generally known as the First Folio.

Shakespeare had never severed his relations with Stratford. His wife and children may sometimes have shared his London lodgings, but their home was Stratford. His son Hamnet was buried there in 1596, and his daughters Susanna and Judith were married there in 1607 and 1616 respectively. (His father, for whom he had secured a coat of arms and thus the privilege of writing himself gentleman, died in 1601, his mother in 1608.) His considerable earnings in London, as actor-sharer, part owner of the Globe, and playwright, were invested chiefly in Stratford property. In 1597 he purchased for £60 New Place, one of the two most imposing residences in the town. A number of other business transactions, as well as minor episodes in his career, have left documentary records. By 1611 he was in a position to retire, and he seems gradually to have withdrawn from theatrical activity in order to live in Stratford. In March, 1616, he made a will, leaving token bequests to Burbage, Heminge, and Condell, but the bulk of his estate to his family. The most famous feature of the will, the bequest of the second-best bed to his wife, reveals nothing about Shakespeare's marriage; the quaintness of the provision seems commonplace to those familiar with ancient testaments. Shakespeare died April 23, 1616, and was buried in the Stratford church where he had been christened. Within seven years a monument was erected to his memory on the north wall of the chancel. Its portrait bust and the Droeshout engraving on the title page of the First Folio provide the only likenesses with an established claim to authenticity. The best verbal vignette was written by his rival Ben Jonson, the more impressive for being imbedded in a context mainly critical :

. . . I loved the man, and doe honour his memory (on this side idolatry) as much as any. Hee was indeed honest, and of an open and free nature: had an excellent Phantsie, brave notions, and gentle expressions. . . . (*Timber or Discoveries*, ca. 1623–30)

*

The reader of Shakespeare's plays is aided by a general knowledge of the way in which they were staged. The King's men acquired a roofed and artificially lighted theatre only toward the close of Shakespeare's career, and then only for winter use. Nearly all his plays were designed for performance in such structures as the Globe – a three-tiered amphitheatre with a large rectangular platform extending to the center of its yard. The plays were staged by daylight, by large casts brilliantly costumed, but with only a minimum of properties, without scenery, and quite possibly without intermissions. There was a rear stage gallery for action "above," and a curtained rear recess for "discoveries" and other special effects, but by far the major portion of any play was enacted upon the projecting platform, with episode following episode in swift succession, and with shifts of time and place signaled the audience only by the momentary clearing of the stage between the episodes. Information about the identity of the characters and, when necessary, about the time and place of the action was incorporated in the dialogue. No place-headings have been inserted in the present editions; these are apt to obscure the original fluidity of structure, with the emphasis upon action and speech rather than scenic background. (Indications of place are supplied in the footnotes.) The acting, including that of the youthful apprentices to the profession who performed the parts of women, was highly skillful, with a premium placed upon grace of gesture and beauty of diction. The audiences, a cross section of the general public, commonly numbered a thousand, sometimes more than two thousand. Judged by the type of plays they applauded, these audiences were not only large but also perceptive.

THE TEXTS OF THE PLAYS

About half of Shakespeare's plays appeared in print for the first time in the folio volume of 1623. The others had been published individually, usually in quarto volumes, during his lifetime or in the six years following his death. The copy used by the printers of the quartos varied greatly in merit, sometimes representing Shakespeare's true text, sometimes only a debased version of that text. The copy used by the printers of the folio also varied in merit, but was chosen with care. Since it consisted of the best available manuscripts, or the more acceptable quartos (although frequently in editions other than the first), or of quartos corrected by reference to manuscripts, we have good or reasonably good texts of most of the thirty-seven plays.

In the present series, the plays have been newly edited from quarto or folio texts, depending, when a choice offered, upon which is now regarded by bibliographical specialists as the more authoritative. The ideal has been to reproduce the chosen texts with as few alterations as possible, beyond occasional relineation, expansion of abbreviations, and modernization of punctuation and spelling. Emendation is held to a minimum, and such material as has been added, in the way of stage directions and lines supplied by an alternative text, has been enclosed in square brackets.

None of the plays printed in Shakespeare's lifetime were divided into acts and scenes, and the inference is that the author's own manuscripts were not so divided. In the folio collection, some of the plays remained undivided, some were divided into acts, and some were divided into acts and scenes. During the eighteenth century all of the plays were divided into acts and scenes, and in the Cambridge edition of the mid-nineteenth century, from which the influential Globe text derived, this division was more or less regularized and the lines were numbered. Many useful works of reference employ the act–scene–line apparatus thus established.

Since this act–scene division is obviously convenient, but is of very dubious authority so far as Shakespeare's own structural principles are concerned, or the original manner of staging his plays, a problem is presented to modern editors. In the present series the act–scene division is retained marginally, and may be viewed as a reference aid like the line numbering. A star marks the points of division when these points have been determined by a cleared stage indicating a shift of time and place in the action of the play, or when no harm results from the editorial assumption that there is such a shift. However, at those points where the established division is clearly misleading – that is, where continuous action has been split up into separate "scenes" – the star is omitted and the distortion corrected. This mechanical expedient seemed the best means of combining utility and accuracy.

THE GENERAL EDITOR

INTRODUCTION

This play, which must have seen its first performance in 1608 or thereabouts, may be the last of Shakespeare's tragedies as we define them to-day. Criticism has tended to range it beside his greatest for its power, its amplitude, and its craftsmanship. But it has never been so popular as the others; and that is by no means surprising, since it so expressly calls into question the equivocal values of popularity. On an elementary human basis, Shakespeare's appeal has always been exerted through his characters, and through the bonds of sympathy that ally them with the spectator or the reader. From the outset of *Coriolanus*, however, such an identification is harshly repelled; and modern ideology, which disposes us to sympathize less readily with the hero than with the viewpoint of his antagonists, has slanted and colored our understanding of both. Yet recent history, by grimly reviving the very issues that Shakespeare dramatized, has greatly increased the importance and the impressiveness of his dramatization. *Coriolanus* has been found, on revival, to be more fraught with significance for our time than any other drama in the Shakespearean repertory. Max Reinhardt's production in Germany was turbulently prophetic. French crowds rioted when, in the years between the wars, it was performed at the Comédie Française.

Shakespeare's audiences, on occasion, could be quite as explosive. His England must often have seemed to be rifted internally, as well as externally menaced. Even while he was writing *Coriolanus,* outcries over the scarcity of grain were daily reaching London from the Midlands. A Stuart monarch, recently enthroned, claimed more and wielded less authority than his Tudor predecessors had done. Strong-willed men could make spectacular bids for power; Sir Walter Ralegh was being held in the Tower on charges of conspiracy; the Earl of Essex had incited Londoners to fight in the streets a few years before; and for that insurrection *Richard II* had been utilized as propaganda. Such, of course, had not been Shakespeare's purpose. His mounting sequence of histories had made England's coming-of-age coincide with his own, and had subsumed – along with the English past – the most triumphant decade of the first Elizabeth's reign. Therefore his chronicle plays had been somewhat controlled by considerations of patriotism, royal prerogative, and the relative familiarity of the facts. Seeking a freer field of political observation, pushing toward profounder formulations of statecraft, shifting his concern from the ruler's duties and rights to those of the citizen, Shakespeare was inevitably led to a point where more distant roads converge: the archetype of city-states, the keystone of western traditions, Rome.

At the beginning of his tragic period – the opening years of the seventeenth century – he essayed this republican theme in *Julius Caesar.* He resumed it with an even grander sequel, *Antony and Cleopatra,* but not until after completing his exhaustive explorations of personality in *Hamlet, Othello, Macbeth,* and *King Lear.* Thus *Coriolanus* rounds out a trilogy, though it stands somewhat apart from the other two Roman plays, possibly nearer to *Antony and Cleopatra* in scope and to *Julius Caesar* in subject. All three, taken together, constitute a great debate on ethics, in which the statement of private interests is balanced against the counter-statement of public responsibilities. *Julius Caesar* lays the dialectical groundwork by showing a group of individuals in conflict over the state. *Antony and Cleopatra* shows its individualistic hero and heroine rejecting their obligations to their respective states and behaving as if they were laws unto themselves. *Coriolanus* explores the extreme situation of the individual who pits himself against the state. Here Julius Caesar might have proved a monumental counterpart; but Shakespeare's portrait was brief and enigmatic, registering the impact of Caesarism on others, notably on the conscience of Marcus Brutus; and Brutus, acting in the "common good to all," presented the obverse of the Roman coin whereon Coriolanus is stamped incisively.

The historical Caius Marcius Coriolanus, figuring in the earliest annals of the Republic, had won his victory at Corioli in 493 B.C. He may indeed have been a half-legendary embodiment of patrician resistance to the increasing demands of the plebeians and especially their newly appointed spokesmen, the tribunes. Hence, instead of being elected to the consulate, he was banished, and went over to the enemy as the hero does in the play. In the end, as the historian Mommsen sums it up, "he expiated his first treason by a second, and both by death." Poetic justice was better served than either side. Shakespeare drew his version of these episodes from Plutarch's *Lives*, the source that inspired him most, that treasury of ancient biography which comprises a series of comparative studies in heroic citizenship. Plutarch, the Greek moralist, saw Coriolanus as an outstanding example of the peculiarly Roman conception of virtue: *virtus*, which is translated "valiantness." The vice that attended and finally defeated this salient quality was "willfulness." Plutarch's contrasting parallel is the career of Alcibiades, whose ingratiating suppleness – like Antony's – throws the intransigent arrogance of Coriolanus into bold relief. That the latter was brought up by his widowed mother, and was chiefly animated by the desire to please her, Plutarch is at pains to emphasize.

Shakespeare follows Plutarch so very closely that he

often echoes the phraseology of the magnificent Elizabethan translation by Sir Thomas North. Volumnia's plea to her son in Act V, eloquently massive as it is, is scarcely more than a metrical adaptation of North's prose. On the other hand, her appeal to him in Act III is Shakespeare's interpolation; he has reserved his right to modify and augment his material in the interests of psychological motivation and dramatic equilibrium; and those two interventions of Volumnia, in each case changing the mind of Coriolanus, are the turning-points of the plot. Rhetoric, the art of persuasion, determined not only the style but also the structure of *Julius Caesar*: Cassius persuades Brutus, Brutus persuades the people, Mark Antony persuades them otherwise. *Coriolanus* is not less Roman in its recourse to public speech; and speech-making triumphs ironically over war-mongering; but now the forensic mode is that of dissuasion. The candidate actually dissuades the people from voting for him; the general at length is dissuaded from pursuing his revenge. His vein is negation: curses, threats, and invectives from first to last. Once he rallies his men; many times he scolds them. When he girds the gods, his rant sounds more like the misanthropic Timon than the iconoclastic Tamburlaine. Yet how narrowly it misses the tone of Hotspur!

Coriolanus to the contrary, the word is not "mildly." The language of the play reverberates with the dissonance of its subject-matter and the thunder-like percussion of its protagonist. The words are so tensely involved in the situation that they do not lend themselves much to purple passages or quotations out of context. Reflecting a stylistic transition, they seem to combine the serried diction of Shakespeare's middle period with the flowing rhythm of his later plays. The speeches frequently begin and break off in the middle of a line; but the cadence of the blank verse persists through occasional setbacks; and sometimes the overlapping pentameters are more evident to the ear than on the page. This has been a problem for editors, many of whom have regarded the difficulties of the text as invitations to change it. The present edition assumes that the unique redaction of *Coriolanus*, which has come down to us through the folios, is more or less authoritative; and that, except for some obvious readjustments and a few unavoidable emendations, it simply needs to be modernized in spelling and punctuation. The original stage directions, which are unusually explicit, convey a suggestion of pageantry commanding the full resources of the resplendent Globe. And from a contemporary sketch of *Titus Andronicus*, we know that the Elizabethans could approximate Roman dress.

Though the scenes march by in swift continuity, moving from camp to camp and faction to faction, the acts are sharply divided, as if to stress the division among the characters. Act I presents the hero in his proper field of action, the battlefield, where heroism can be demonstrated in its simplest terms as valiantness. Act II brings him reluctantly home to his triumph, and even more grudgingly into the electoral campaign. This goes against him in Act III and leads, after another disastrous attempt at propitiation, to the decree of banishment. Act IV pursues the exiled Coriolanus traversing the distance between Rome and Antium, and betraying himself and his fellow Romans to the Volscian general, Aufidius. Act V witnesses his capitulation and consummates his tragedy: military commitment, resisting civic pressure, yields to domestic. Throughout these vicissitudes he sustains his predominating role, the central figure when he is on stage, the topic of discussion when he is not. His monolithic character is measured by no single foil of comparable stature – least of all by his rival, Aufidius, who has failed to square accounts with him honorably, and vowed to do so through dishonorable means if necessary – but by his dynamic relations with all the others, on the diverging levels of family, city, and enemy.

The one is accordingly weighed against the many; and

the tendency toward monodrama is counterpoised by an unusual number of choric roles – citizens, officers, soldiers, servants, other ranks of society. The scales tip during the roadside interview between a Roman and a Volscian, with its implication that Coriolanus is taking the same road to espionage and betrayal. As for the populace, the tribunes can hardly speak for it because it is so vocal on its own behalf; the mistake of Coriolanus is to believe that its "voices" are merely votes. Generalization soon breaks down into Hob and Dick, and the types are individualized, loudly insisting upon their individuality. There are some ugly mob-scenes and one violent outbreak of street-fighting, but mother-wit is the characteristic weapon The humorous mediator, Menenius Agrippa, can handle this pithy prose idiom. The crowd in turn can rise to the pitch of blank verse, while their shrewd heckling enlivens his tale of the belly and the members. The First Citizen, "great toe" though he may be, accepts the question-begging metaphor that identifies the organ of digestion with the deliberation of the Senate. But, logically enough, he presses the claims of the other parts, including the soldierly arm. The parable will apply to the choleric hero as much as to the angry mob.

In a subsequent argument, when Coriolanus is compared to a disease, Menenius retorts that he is rather a diseased limb which can be cured. By this time many sores and wounds have been metaphorically and literally probed, thereby revealing other aspects of the body politic. The age-old fable expounded by Menenius, appeasing the uproar of the introductory scene, has served to establish an ideal of social order – the concept of commonweal, *res publica* – more honored in the breach than the observance. It has also concretely grounded the imagery of the play in the matter at hand, the dearth of corn, the fundamental problem of nourishment. The struggling classes seek to feed on each other; Menenius is a self-confessed epicure; the poor justify themselves by hungry proverbs, and

Coriolanus finds himself in their desperate position when he appears at the feast of Aufidius. In close association with these images of food, battle is described as if it were harvest, with the swords of destruction figuratively turning into the ploughshares of fertility. Another associated train of thought runs to animals, always an inspiration for name-calling. The hero is introduced as a dog to the people, who are curs to him then and crucially later. The prevailing code is dog-eat-dog.

Menenius points the moral succinctly when he demands: "On both sides more respect." Since both sides indulge in such embittered polemics, interpretation has varied between the extremes of left and right, now underlining the dangers of dictatorship and now the weaknesses of democracy, according to the political adherence of the interpreters. Nothing could better attest what Coleridge, in this connection, called "the wonderful philosophic impartiality in Shakespeare's politics." His portrayal of the multitude, whose sedition he arms with a grievance, is anti-demagogic rather than anti-democratic. The demagogues are the tribunes, portrayed in unequivocal cynicism, dissuading the plebs from the suffrage they have already pledged to Coriolanus. Coriolanus, on his side, is no friend of the people; and it is to the credit of his integrity that he cannot act a part he does not feel. He earns, with an authoritarian vengeance, the title that Ibsen would bestow in irony upon his humanitarian Dr Stockmann – *An Enemy of the People*. All men are enemies, rivals if not foes, to Coriolanus. His aggressive temperament could never be happy until it had lurched all other swords of the garland. His fight against the world is not for booty nor praise nor office, but for acknowledged superiority; he does not want to dominate but to excel; and he cannot bear the thought of subordination.

We need not look far afield for the school that nurtured that spirit of single-minded competitiveness. The Roman matron, the masculine dowager, the statuesque Volumnia, is both father and mother to her son; and she has taught him aristocratic scorn along with martial courage. His wife, the gracious Virgilia, in contrast is sheer femininity; and her main attribute, like Cordelia's, is silence. His young son chases butterflies with congenital resolution; subsequently Coriolanus commands a Volscian army as eager as boys chasing butterflies. No man can withstand him and only one woman can plead with him. In yielding to her, in feeling this ultimate modicum of feminine tenderness, the strong man becomes again – as it were – a child. Thence the sting in the last taunt of Aufidius. Under the epithet "traitor" Coriolanus has slightly flinched. But "boy!" "Thou boy of tears!" In significant contradistinction, we are reminded continually that the tribunes are elderly men. Leadership, as Volumnia's boy had learned it in the wars, was largely an individual matter of athletic prowess, having little to do with the sort of maturity that peaceful civilian government requires. Perhaps the trouble, as analyzed by Aufidius, lay in a soldier's inability to move "from th' casque to th' cushion." The virtues of war may well be the vices of peace; the man on horseback, dismounted, a sorry creature.

T. S. Eliot's modernized *Coriolan* consists of two poems: "Triumphal March" and "Difficulties of a Statesman." These headings suggest the dilemma of Shakespeare's protagonist. His is not an internal struggle; so far as his two short soliloquies indicate, the treason causes him less mental anguish than the election; and, what is even worse, at Antium he employs the flatteries he has despised at Rome. Rather it is the external manifestation of his colossal pride that exalts him, all but deifies him, and renders the slippery turns of fortune more precipitous than the Tarpeian Rock. "Rome or I! One or the other must fall!" Such is the climax, verbalized by Wagner, to Beethoven's orchestration of this theme. "The note of banishment," the note that James Joyce kept hearing in Shakespeare's plays, is never more plangently sounded than in the parting denunciation of Coriolanus to the Romans: "I banish you!" Never was man more alienated than he, as the gates of Rome close behind him and he is forced to seek "a world elsewhere." The scene reverses his initial triumph, when the gates of Corioli shut him in alone of all the Romans. The ironic pattern is completed, on his return to the hostile town, by his fatal words to its citizens. And note the emphatic position of the first personal pronoun:

> If you have writ your annals true, 'tis there
> That, like an eagle in a dovecote, I
> Fluttered your Volscians in Corioles.
> Alone I did it.

Othello, at a similar moment, had the satisfaction of recalling his services to the state. Caius Marcius – Coriolanus no longer – can only glory in his isolation. The word "alone" is repeated more than in any other Shakespearean work; and, from the welter of similes, the most memorable is "a lonely dragon." We end by realizing the ambiguity of the foreign name this Roman has proudly flaunted. How can he expect it to be anything but a target of hatred for the orphans and widows and comrades-in-arms of men he has killed? After the combat in which he gained it, he had generously tried to befriend a certain Volscian, and had characteristically forgotten the poor man's name – a touch which Shakespeare added to Plutarch's anecdote. Shakespeare's insight, detailed as it is, confirms an observation cited from Plato by Plutarch: that such overriding egoism can only terminate in "desolation." This must be that desolation of solitude which the American imagination has paralleled in the career of another tragic captain, Melville's Ahab.

Harvard University   HARRY LEVIN

NOTE ON THE TEXT

Coriolanus was first published in the folio of 1623, evidently from the author's own manuscript. The present edition follows the folio text, with emendation confined as a rule to the most generally recognized instances of misprinting and mislineation. The folio text is divided into acts but not into scenes. The division provided marginally for reference in the present edition represents the folio acts as divided into scenes by later editors. This play is exceptional in the large number of speakers given only generic names in the speech-prefixes. These have been spelled out *First Citizen* etc. instead of *1. Citizen* etc. as in the other plays of the present edition. All material departures from the folio text are listed below, with the adopted reading in italics followed by the folio reading in roman.

I, i, 60 *First Citizen* 2 Cit. (and so through rest of scene)   62 *you.* For you for   105 *tauntingly* taintingly   110 *crownèd* crown'd   179 *vile* vilde   209 *Shouting* Shooting   221 s.d. *Junius* Annius   234 *Lartius* Lucius   239, 243 *First Senator* Sen.
I, ii, 4 *on* one
I, iii, 34 *that's* that   81 *Ithaca* Athica   108 s.d. *Exeunt* Exeunt Ladies
I, iv, 42 *Follow me* followes   45 s.d. *gates* Gati   57 *Cato's* Calues
I, v, 3 s.d. *Alarum* exeunt. Alarum   *Titus Lartius* Titus
I, vi, 24 s.d. *Enter Marcius* (at l. 21 in F)   32 *burned* burnt   53 *Antiates* Antients   70 *Lesser* Lessen   81 *select* select from all
I, vii, 7 s.d. *Exeunt* Exit
I, ix, s.d. *Flourish* (not in F)   46 *coverture* Ouerture   49 *shout* shoot   66 *All* Omnes   *Caius Marcius* Marcus Caius   67, 78, 81, 89 *Coriolanus* Martius
I, x, 2, 16, 29, 33 *First Soldier* Sould   22 *Embargements* Embarquements
II, i, 16 *with all* withall   52 *cannot* can   57 *you you* you   59 *bisson* beesome   155 *Coriolanus* Martius Caius Coriolanus   179 *relish* Rallish   193 s.d. *Brutus . . . forward* Enter Brutus and Sicinius   244 *touch* teach   249 *to th'* to the
II, ii, 44 *Caius Marcius* Martius Caius   65, 121, 128 *First Senator* Senat   79 *one on's* on ones   89 *chin* Shinne   90 *bristled* brizled   106 *took. From face to foot* tooke from face to foote :   136 *suffrage* sufferage   152 *Senators* Senat   s.d. *Manent* Manet

23

II, iii, 26 *wedged* wadg'd   35 *it. I say, if* it, I say. If   39 *all to-gether* altogether   59 s.d. *Enter . . . Citizens* (at l. 58 in F)   65 *not* but   84, 87, 101 *Fourth Citizen* 1.   100 *Fifth Citizen* 2.   109 *hire* higher   110 *toge* tongue   113 *do't,* doo't?   116 *t' o'erpeer* to or'epeere   121, 125 *voices!* voyces?   221 *th'* the   238 *And Censorinus nobly* And nobly   *naméd* nam'd   239 *being by the people chosen* being chosen

III, i, s.d. *Lartius* Latius   10 *vilely* vildly   63, 75 *First Senator* Senat.   91 *O good* O God!   143 *Where one* Whereon   172 s.d. *Enter an Aedile* (at l. 171 in F)   185 *All* (at l. 187 in F)   198, 233, 335 *First Senator* Sena.   231 *Coriolanus* Com.   237 *Cominius* Corio.   238 *Coriolanus* Mene.   287 *our* one   305 *Sicinius* Menen.   323 *bring him* bring him in peace

III, ii, 13 s.d. *Enter Volumnia* (at l. 6 in F)   25 *taxings* things   26 *First Senator* Sen.   32 *herd* heart   101 *bear? Well, I* beare Well? I   115 *lulls* lull

III, iii, 32 *for th'* fourth   36 *Throng* Through   55 *accents* Actions   99 *i' th' name* In the Name   110 *for* from   136 s.d. *Menenius Cumalijs*   138 *Hoo! hoo!* Hoo, oo.

IV, i, 34 *wilt* will

IV, ii, 9 s.d. *Enter . . . Menenius* (at l. 7 in F)   36 *let us* let's   44 s.d. *Exeunt* Exit   53 *Exeunt* (at end of preceding speech in F, with *Exit* here)

IV, iii, 31 *will* well

IV, iv, 23 *hate* haue

IV, v, 108 *thy* that   151 *strucken* strocken   164 *on* one   178 *lief* liue   203 *sowl* sole   225 *sprightly, waking* spightly walking   227 *sleepy* sleepe   229 *war* warres

IV, vi, 10 s.d. *Enter Menenius* (at l. 9 in F)   25 *Citizens* All

IV, vii, 15 *Had* haue   37 *'twas* 'was   49 *virtues* Vertue   55 *founder* fouler

V, i, 41 *toward* towards

V, ii, s.d. *on* or   16 *haply* happely   56 s.d. *and* with   58 *errand* arrant   61 *by my* my   72 *our* your   83 *pity note* pitty: Note   90 s.d. *Manent* Manet

V, iii, 48 *prate* pray   56 *What is* What's   63 *holp* hope   79 *you'd* youl'd   149 *fine* fiue   154 *noble man* Nobleman   163 *clucked* clock'd   169 *him* him with him   179 *this* his

V, v, 4 *Unshout* Unshoot

V, vi, 48 s.d. *sound* sounds   72 *That* Then,   99 *other* others   114 *Fluttered* Flatter'd   115 *it. Boy?* it, Boy.   129 s.d. *Draw* Draw both   *kill* kils   153 s.d. *Coriolanus* Martius

CORIOLANUS

Caius Marcius, afterwards Caius Marcius Coriolanus
Titus Lartius
Cominius } Generals against the Volscians
Menenius Agrippa, friend to Coriolanus
Sicinius Velutus
Junius Brutus } Tribunes of the People
Young Marcius, son to Coriolanus
Nicanor, a Roman
Senators
Officers
Aediles
Heralds } of Rome
Messengers
Soldiers
Citizens of Rome
Tullus Aufidius, General of the Volscians
Adrian, a Volscian
Lieutenant to Aufidius
Conspirators with Aufidius
Servants to Aufidius
Senators
Lords } of Corioli
Soldiers
A Citizen of Antium
Volumnia, mother to Coriolanus
Virgilia, wife to Coriolanus
Valeria, friend to Virgilia
Gentlewoman, attending on Virgilia

Scene : Rome and the neighborhood ;
the Volscian towns of Corioli and Antium]

CORIOLANUS

Enter a company of mutinous Citizens, with staves,   I, i
clubs, and other weapons.

FIRST CITIZEN Before we proceed any further, hear me
speak.

ALL Speak, speak.

FIRST CITIZEN You are all resolved rather to die than to
famish?

ALL Resolved, resolved.

FIRST CITIZEN First, you know Caius Marcius is chief
enemy to the people.

ALL We know't, we know't.

FIRST CITIZEN Let us kill him, and we'll have corn at
our own price. Is't a verdict?   10

ALL No more talking on't! Let it be done! Away, away!   11

SECOND CITIZEN One word, good citizens.

FIRST CITIZEN We are accounted poor citizens, the
patricians good. What authority surfeits on would re- 14
lieve us. If they would yield us but the superfluity while 15
it were wholesome, we might guess they relieved us
humanely; but they think we are too dear. The leanness 17
that afflicts us, the object of our misery, is as an in- 18
ventory to particularize their abundance; our sufferance 19
is a gain to them. Let us revenge this with our pikes ere 20

I, i A street in Rome   **10** *verdict* agreement   **11** *on't* about it   **14** *patri-cians* aristocrats; *good* substantial; *authority* the ruling class   **15** *super-fluity* surplus   **17** *dear* expensive   **18** *object* spectacle   **19** *sufferance* suffering   **20** *pikes* pitchforks

27

21 we become rakes; for the gods know I speak this in hunger for bread, not in thirst for revenge.

SECOND CITIZEN Would you proceed especially against Caius Marcius?

FIRST CITIZEN Against him first. He's a very dog to the
26 commonalty.

SECOND CITIZEN Consider you what services he has done for his country?

FIRST CITIZEN Very well, and could be content to give him good report for't, but that he pays himself with being proud.

SECOND CITIZEN Nay, but speak not maliciously.

FIRST CITIZEN I say unto you, what he hath done
34 famously, he did it to that end. Though soft-conscienced men can be content to say it was for his country, he did it to please his mother and to be partly proud, which he
37 is, even to the altitude of his virtue.

SECOND CITIZEN What he cannot help in his nature, you account a vice in him. You must in no way say he is covetous.

FIRST CITIZEN If I must not, I need not be barren of accusations. He hath faults, with surplus, to tire in repetition.
    Shouts within.
What shouts are these? The other side o' th' city is risen.
44 Why stay we prating here? To th' Capitol!

ALL Come, come!

46 FIRST CITIZEN Soft! who comes here?
    Enter Menenius Agrippa.

SECOND CITIZEN Worthy Menenius Agrippa, one that hath always loved the people.

FIRST CITIZEN He's one honest enough. Would all the rest were so!

---

21 *rakes* lean as rakes   26 *commonalty* common people   34 *to that end* i.e. to achieve fame   37 *altitude of his virtue* height of his valor   44 *Capitol* Temple of Jupiter, Capitoline Hill   46 *Soft* stay

MENENIUS
  What work's, my countrymen, in hand? Where go you
  With bats and clubs? The matter? Speak, I pray you.
FIRST CITIZEN Our business is not unknown to th'
  Senate. They have had inkling this fortnight what we
  intend to do, which now we'll show 'em in deeds. They
  say poor suitors have strong breaths; they shall know 56
  we have strong arms too.
MENENIUS
  Why, masters, my good friends, mine honest neighbors,
  Will you undo yourselves?
FIRST CITIZEN We cannot, sir, we are undone already.
MENENIUS
  I tell you, friends, most charitable care
  Have the patricians of you. For your wants,   62
  Your suffering in this dearth, you may as well   63
  Strike at the heaven with your staves as lift them
  Against the Roman state, whose course will on   65
  The way it takes, cracking ten thousand curbs
  Of more strong link asunder than can ever
  Appear in your impediment. For the dearth,   68
  The gods, not the patricians, make it, and
  Your knees to them, not arms, must help. Alack,
  You are transported by calamity   71
  Thither where more attends you, and you slander
  The helms o' th' state, who care for you like fathers,   73
  When you curse them as enemies.
FIRST CITIZEN Care for us? True, indeed! They ne'er
  cared for us yet: suffer us to famish, and their store-
  houses crammed with grain; make edicts for usury, to
  support usurers; repeal daily any wholesome act estab-
  lished against the rich, and provide more piercing   79
  statutes daily to chain up and restrain the poor. If the

56 *suitors* petitioners 62 *For* as for 63 *dearth* famine 65 *on* go on
68 *your impediment* the obstruction you raise 71 *transported* carried
away 73 *helms* pilots 79 *piercing* far-reaching

wars eat us not up, they will; and there's all the love
they bear us.

MENENIUS
Either you must
83   Confess yourselves wondrous malicious,
Or be accused of folly. I shall tell you
A pretty tale. It may be you have heard it;
But, since it serves my purpose, I will venture
87   To stale't a little more.

FIRST CITIZEN Well, I'll hear it, sir; yet you must not
89   think to fob off our disgrace with a tale. But, an't please
you, deliver.

MENENIUS
There was a time when all the body's members
Rebelled against the belly, thus accused it:
That only like a gulf it did remain
I' th' midst o' th' body, idle and unactive,
95   Still cupboarding the viand, never bearing
96   Like labor with the rest, where th' other instruments
Did see and hear, devise, instruct, walk, feel,
98   And mutually participate, did minister
99   Unto the appetite and affection common
Of the whole body. The belly answered –

FIRST CITIZEN Well, sir, what answer made the belly?

MENENIUS
Sir, I shall tell you. With a kind of smile,
103   Which ne'er came from the lungs, but even thus –
For, look you, I may make the belly smile
As well as speak – it tauntingly replied
To th' discontented members, the mutinous parts
107   That envied his receipt; even so most fitly
108   As you malign our senators, for that
They are not such as you.

---

83 *wondrous* extraordinarily 87 *stale't* make it stale 89 *fob off* elude;
disgrace hardship; *an't* if it 95 *Still* always 96 *Like* similar; *instruments*
organs 98 *participate* taking part 99 *affection* inclination 103 *lungs* i.e.
organ of laughter 107 *his receipt* what he received 108 *for that* because

FIRST CITIZEN   Your belly's answer? What?
The kingly crownèd head, the vigilant eye,
The counsellor heart, the arm our soldier,
Our steed the leg, the tongue our trumpeter,
With other muniments and petty helps   113
In this our fabric, if that they –
MENENIUS   What then?
'Fore me, this fellow speaks! What then? what then?   115
FIRST CITIZEN
Should by the cormorant belly be restrained,
Who is the sink o' th' body –
MENENIUS   Well, what then?
FIRST CITIZEN
The former agents, if they did complain,
What could the belly answer?
MENENIUS   I will tell you;
If you'll bestow a small – of what you have little –
Patience awhile, you'st hear the belly's answer.   121
FIRST CITIZEN
Y' are long about it.   122
MENENIUS   Note me this, good friend;
Your most grave belly was deliberate,   123
Not rash like his accusers, and thus answered:
'True is it, my incorporate friends,' quoth he,
'That I receive the general food at first,
Which you do live upon; and fit it is,
Because I am the storehouse and the shop   128
Of the whole body. But, if you do remember,
I send it through the rivers of your blood
Even to the court, the heart, to th' seat o' th' brain;
And, through the cranks and offices of man,   132
The strongest nerves and small inferior veins
From me receive that natural competency   134

113 *muniments* furnishings 115 *'Fore me* upon my soul 121 *you'st* you'll
(provincial) 122 *Y' are* you're 123 *Your* this 128 *shop* workshop
132 *cranks* windings; *offices* servants' quarters 134 *competency* sufficiency

Whereby they live. And though that all at once' –
You, my good friends! This says the belly. Mark me.

FIRST CITIZEN
Ay, sir, well, well.

MENENIUS   'Though all at once cannot
See what I do deliver out to each,
Yet I can make my audit up, that all
From me do back receive the flour of all,
And leave me but the bran.' What say you to't?

FIRST CITIZEN
It was an answer. How apply you this?

MENENIUS
The senators of Rome are this good belly,
And you the mutinous members. For examine
145 Their counsels and their cares, disgest things rightly
146 Touching the weal o' th' common, you shall find
No public benefit which you receive
But it proceeds or comes from them to you,
And no way from yourselves. What do you think,
You, the great toe of this assembly?

FIRST CITIZEN
I the great toe! Why the great toe?

MENENIUS
For that, being one o' th' lowest, basest, poorest
Of this most wise rebellion, thou goest foremost.
154 Thou rascal, that art worst in blood to run,
155 Lead'st first to win some vantage.
But make you ready your stiff bats and clubs.
Rome and her rats are at the point of battle;
158 The one side must have bale.
   Enter Caius Marcius. Hail, noble Marcius!

MARCIUS
159 Thanks. What's the matter, you dissentious rogues,
That, rubbing the poor itch of your opinion,

---

145 *disgest* digest 146 *weal o' th' common* public welfare 154 *rascal*
worthless deer; *blood* condition 155 *vantage* advantage 158 *bale* destruction 159 *dissentious* seditious

Make yourselves scabs?

FIRST CITIZEN   We have ever your good word.

MARCIUS

He that will give good words to thee will flatter
Beneath abhorring. What would you have, you curs,
That like nor peace nor war? The one affrights you,   164
The other makes you proud. He that trusts to you,   165
Where he should find you lions, finds you hares;
Where foxes, geese. You are no surer, no,
Than is the coal of fire upon the ice,
Or hailstone in the sun. Your virtue is
To make him worthy whose offense subdues him   170
And curse that justice did it. Who deserves greatness   171
Deserves your hate; and your affections are
A sick man's appetite, who desires most that
Which would increase his evil. He that depends
Upon your favors swims with fins of lead
And hews down oaks with rushes. Hang ye! Trust ye?
With every minute you do change a mind,
And call him noble that was now your hate,
Him vile that was your garland. What's the matter,
That in these several places of the city
You cry against the noble Senate, who,
Under the gods, keep you in awe, which else
Would feed on one another? What's their seeking?   183

MENENIUS

For corn at their own rates, whereof they say
The city is well stored.

MARCIUS   Hang 'em! They say?
They'll sit by th' fire and presume to know
What's done i' th' Capitol, who's like to rise,
Who thrives and who declines; side factions and give 188
  out
Conjectural marriages, making parties strong

---

164 *nor . . . nor* neither . . . nor; *The one* i.e. war   165 *The other* i.e. peace
170 *make him worthy* glorify that man; *subdues* degrades   171 *that justice*
that justice which   183 *seeking* petition   188 *side* take sides with

190   And feebling such as stand not in their liking
191   Below their cobbled shoes. They say there's grain
         enough?
192   Would the nobility lay aside their ruth,
193   And let me use my sword, I'd make a quarry
194   With thousands of these quartered slaves as high
195   As I could pick my lance.

MENENIUS
      Nay, these are almost thoroughly persuaded;
      For though abundantly they lack discretion,
198   Yet are they passing cowardly. But, I beseech you,
      What says the other troop?

MARCIUS   They are dissolved. Hang 'em!
200   They said they were anhungry, sighed forth proverbs –
      That hunger broke stone walls, that dogs must eat,
      That meat was made for mouths, that the gods sent not
      Corn for the rich men only. With these shreds
      They vented their complainings, which being answered
      And a petition granted them, a strange one,
206   To break the heart of generosity,
      And make bold power look pale, they threw their caps
      As they would hang them on the horns o' th' moon,
209   Shouting their emulation.

MENENIUS   What is granted them?

MARCIUS
210   Five tribunes to defend their vulgar wisdoms,
      Of their own choice. One's Junius Brutus,
212   Sicinius Velutus, and I know not – 'Sdeath!
      The rabble should have first unroofed the city
      Ere so prevailed with me; it will in time
215   Win upon power, and throw forth greater themes

190 *feebling* making weak   191 *cobbled* mended   192 *ruth* pity   193
quarry heap of slaughtered   194 *quartered* cut in four like criminals   195
pick pitch   198 *passing* extremely   200 *anhungry* hungry   206 *generosity*
aristocracy   209 *emulation* envy   210 *tribunes* official protectors of the
people's interests   212 *'Sdeath* (modified oath)   215 *Win upon power*
gain authority

For insurrection's arguing.   216

MENENIUS   This is strange.
MARCIUS
Go, get you home, you fragments!
Enter a Messenger hastily.

MESSENGER
Where's Caius Marcius?
MARCIUS   Here. What's the matter?
MESSENGER
The news is, sir, the Volsces are in arms.
MARCIUS
I am glad on't. Then we shall ha' means to vent   220
Our musty superfluity. See, our best elders.
*Enter Sicinius Velutus, Junius Brutus, Cominius,
Titus Lartius, with other Senators.*

FIRST SENATOR
Marcius, 'tis true that you have lately told us:
The Volsces are in arms.
MARCIUS   They have a leader,
Tullus Aufidius, that will put you to't.   224
I sin in envying his nobility;
And were I any thing but what I am,
I would wish me only he.
COMINIUS   You have fought together?   227
MARCIUS
Were half to half the world by th' ears and he
Upon my party, I'd revolt, to make   229
Only my wars with him. He is a lion
That I am proud to hunt.
FIRST SENATOR   Then, worthy Marcius,
Attend upon Cominius to these wars.
COMINIUS
It is your former promise.
MARCIUS   Sir, it is,

216 *For insurrection's arguing* for revolution to fight over   220 *vent* get rid of
224 *to't* to the test   227 *together* one another   229 *party* side

35

And I am constant. Titus Lartius, thou
Shalt see me once more strike at Tullus' face.
236　　What, art thou stiff? Stand'st out?

TITUS　　　　　　　　　　　　No, Caius Marcius,
I'll lean upon one crutch and fight with t' other,
Ere stay behind this business.

MENENIUS　　　　　　　　　　O, true-bred!

FIRST SENATOR
Your company to th' Capitol, where I know
240　　Our greatest friends attend us.

TITUS [to Cominius]　　　　　　Lead you on.
　　　　[To Marcius]
Follow Cominius. We must follow you.
242　　Right worthy you priority.

COMINIUS　　　　　　　　　　Noble Marcius!

FIRST SENATOR [to the Citizens]
Hence to your homes, be gone!

MARCIUS　　　　　　　　　　Nay, let them follow.
The Volsces have much corn. Take these rats thither
To gnaw their garners. Worshipful mutineers,
246　　Your valor puts well forth. Pray follow.

　　　　　　　　　　　　　　Exeunt. Citizens steal away.
　　　　　　　　　　　　　　Manent Sicinius and Brutus.

SICINIUS
Was ever man so proud as is this Marcius?

BRUTUS
He has no equal.

SICINIUS
When we were chosen tribunes for the people –

BRUTUS
Marked you his lip and eyes?

SICINIUS　　　　　　　　　　Nay, but his taunts.

BRUTUS
251　　Being moved, he will not spare to gird the gods.

---

236 *Stand'st out* do you keep aloof　240 *attend* await　242 *worthy you
priority* you are worthy of precedence　246 *puts . . . forth* blossoms　251
spare to gird desist from taunting

SICINIUS
  Bemock the modest moon.

BRUTUS
  The present wars devour him. He is grown
  Too proud to be so valiant.

SICINIUS   Such a nature,
  Tickled with good success, disdains the shadow
  Which he treads on at noon. But I do wonder
  His insolence can brook to be commanded
  Under Cominius.

BRUTUS   Fame, at the which he aims,
  In whom already he's well graced, cannot   259
  Better be held nor more attained than by
  A place below the first; for what miscarries
  Shall be the general's fault, though he perform
  To th' utmost of a man, and giddy censure
  Will then cry out of Marcius, 'O, if he
  Had borne the business!'

SICINIUS   Besides, if things go well,
  Opinion, that so sticks on Marcius, shall   266
  Of his demerits rob Cominius.   267

BRUTUS   Come.
  Half all Cominius' honors are to Marcius,   268
  Though Marcius earned them not; and all his faults
  To Marcius shall be honors, though indeed
  In aught he merit not.

SICINIUS   Let's hence and hear
  How the dispatch is made, and in what fashion, 272
  More than his singularity, he goes   273
  Upon this present action.

BRUTUS   Let's along.   *Exeunt.*

*

259 *whom* which 266 *so sticks* is so set 267 *demerits* merits 268 *are to* belong to 272 *dispatch* completion 273 *More than his singularity* personal considerations aside

I, ii   *Enter Tullus Aufidius, with Senators of Corioles.*

FIRST SENATOR

So, your opinion is, Aufidius,

2   That they of Rome are entered in our counsels
And know how we proceed.

AUFIDIUS   Is it not yours?

4   What ever have been thought on in this state,
That could be brought to bodily act ere Rome

6   Had circumvention? 'Tis not four days gone
Since I heard thence. These are the words. I think
I have the letter here. Yes, here it is:

9   'They have pressed a power, but it is not known
Whether for east or west. The dearth is great,
The people mutinous; and it is rumored,
Cominius, Marcius your old enemy,
Who is of Rome worse hated than of you,
And Titus Lartius, a most valiant Roman,
These three lead on this preparation
Whither 'tis bent. Most likely 'tis for you.
Consider of it.'

FIRST SENATOR Our army 's in the field.
We never yet made doubt but Rome was ready
To answer us.

AUFIDIUS   Nor did you think it folly

20   To keep your great pretenses veiled till when
They needs must show themselves, which in the
hatching,

22   It seemed, appeared to Rome. By the discovery

23   We shall be shortened in our aim, which was

24   To take in many towns ere almost Rome
Should know we were afoot.

SECOND SENATOR   Noble Aufidius,
Take your commission; hie you to your bands;

I, ii The senate house in Corioli **2** *entered in* initiated into **4** *What*
what counsels **6** *circumvention* means of foiling **9** *pressed a power* raised
an army **20** *pretenses* designs **22** *appeared* became visible **23** *shortened*
reduced **24** *take in* capture

Let us alone to guard Corioles.
If they set down before's, for the remove   28
Bring up your army; but, I think, you'll find
Th' have not prepared for us.   30
AUFIDIUS   O, doubt not that,
I speak from certainties. Nay more,
Some parcels of their power are forth already,   32
And only hitherward. I leave your honors.
If we and Caius Marcius chance to meet,
'Tis sworn between us we shall ever strike
Till one can do no more.
ALL   The gods assist you!
AUFIDIUS
And keep your honors safe!
FIRST SENATOR   Farewell.
SECOND SENATOR   Farewell.
ALL
Farewell.   *Exeunt omnes.*

*

*Enter Volumnia and Virgilia, mother and wife to
Marcius. They set them down on two low stools   I, iii
and sew.*
VOLUMNIA I pray you, daughter, sing, or express yourself in a more comfortable sort. If my son were my   2
husband, I should freelier rejoice in that absence wherein he won honor than in the embracements of his bed
where he would show most love. When yet he was but
tender-bodied and the only son of my womb, when
youth with comeliness plucked all gaze his way, when   7
for a day of kings' entreaties a mother should not sell
him an hour from her beholding, I, considering how   9
honor would become such a person, that it was no better   10

28 *for the remove* to force their departure   30 *Th'* they   32 *parcels* parts
I, iii Within the house of Marcius   2 *comfortable sort* cheerful manner   7
plucked all gaze attracted the attention of all   9 *from her beholding* out of
her sight   10 *person* body

than picture-like to hang by th' wall, if renown made it
not stir, was pleased to let him seek danger where he
was like to find fame. To a cruel war I sent him, from
14   whence he returned, his brows bound with oak. I tell
thee, daughter, I sprang not more in joy at first hearing
he was a man-child than now in first seeing he had
proved himself a man.

VIRGILIA But had he died in the business, madam, how
then?

VOLUMNIA Then his good report should have been my
son; I therein would have found issue. Hear me profess
sincerely: had I a dozen sons, each in my love alike, and
none less dear than thine and my good Marcius, I had
rather had eleven die nobly for their country than one
23   voluptuously surfeit out of action.

Enter a Gentlewoman.

GENTLEWOMAN
Madam, the Lady Valeria is come to visit you.

VIRGILIA
25   Beseech you, give me leave to retire myself.

VOLUMNIA
Indeed, you shall not.
Methinks I hear hither your husband's drum;
See him pluck Aufidius down by th' hair;
As children from a bear, the Volsces shunning him.
Methinks I see him stamp thus, and call thus:
31   'Come on, you cowards! You were got in fear,
Though you were born in Rome.' His bloody brow
With his mailed hand then wiping, forth he goes,
34   Like to a harvest-man that's tasked to mow
35   Or all or lose his hire.

VIRGILIA
His bloody brow? O Jupiter, no blood!

---

14 *bound with oak* crowned for saving a Roman citizen in battle   23 *surfeit*
overindulge himself   25 *Beseech* I beseech   31 *got* begotten   34 *tasked*
employed   35 *Or . . . or* either . . . or

40

VOLUMNIA

    Away, you fool! it more becomes a man

    Than gilt his trophy. The breasts of Hecuba,   38

    When she did suckle Hector, looked not lovelier   39

    Than Hector's forehead when it spit forth blood

    At Grecian sword, contemning. Tell Valeria,   41

    We are fit to bid her welcome.   *Exit Gentlewoman.*

VIRGILIA

    Heavens bless my lord from fell Aufidius!   43

VOLUMNIA

    He'll beat Aufidius' head below his knee

    And tread upon his neck.

      Enter Valeria, with an Usher and a Gentlewoman.

VALERIA My ladies both, good day to you.

VOLUMNIA Sweet madam.

VIRGILIA I am glad to see your ladyship.

VALERIA How do you both? You are manifest house-   49
keepers. What are you sewing here? A fine spot, in good   50
faith. How does your little son?

VIRGILIA I thank your ladyship; well, good madam.

VOLUMNIA He had rather see the swords and hear a drum
than look upon his schoolmaster.

VALERIA O' my word, the father's son! I'll swear 'tis a   55
very pretty boy. O' my troth, I looked upon him o'
Wednesday half an hour together. 'Has such a con-   57
firmed countenance! I saw him run after a gilded
butterfly, and when he caught it, he let it go again, and
after it again, and over and over he comes, and up
again; catched it again; or whether his fall enraged him,
or how 'twas, he did so set his teeth and tear it! O, I
I warrant, how he mammocked it!   62

---

38 *gilt his trophy* gilding becomes his monument; *Hecuba* queen of Troy
39 *Hector* Trojan champion   **41** *contemning* despising   **43** *bless* protect
49–50 *manifest house-keepers* well known for staying at home   **50** *spot* em-
broidered figure   **55** *O'* on   **57** *confirmed* resolute   **62** *mammocked* tore to
pieces

VOLUMNIA One on's father's moods.

VALERIA Indeed, la, 'tis a noble child.

65 VIRGILIA A crack, madam.

VALERIA Come, lay aside your stitchery. I must have you play the idle housewife with me this afternoon.

VIRGILIA No, good madam, I will not out of doors.

VALERIA Not out of doors?

VOLUMNIA She shall, she shall.

VIRGILIA Indeed, no, by your patience. I'll not over the threshold till my lord return from the wars.

VALERIA Fie, you confine yourself most unreasonably.
74   Come, you must go visit the good lady that lies in.

VIRGILIA I will wish her speedy strength and visit her with my prayers, but I cannot go thither.

VOLUMNIA Why, I pray you?

78 VIRGILIA 'Tis not to save labor, nor that I want love.

79 VALERIA You would be another Penelope; yet they say all the yarn she spun in Ulysses' absence did but fill Ithaca full of moths. Come; I would your cambric were
82   sensible as your finger, that you might leave pricking it for pity. Come, you shall go with us.

VIRGILIA No, good madam, pardon me; indeed I will not forth.

VALERIA In truth, la, go with me, and I'll tell you excellent news of your husband.

VIRGILIA O, good madam, there can be none yet.

VALERIA Verily, I do not jest with you. There came news from him last night.

VIRGILIA Indeed, madam?

VALERIA In earnest, it's true; I heard a senator speak it. Thus it is: the Volsces have an army forth, against whom Cominius the general is gone, with one part of our Roman power. Your lord and Titus Lartius are set down before their city Corioles. They nothing doubt

---

65 *crack* imp 74 *lies in* expects a child 78 *want* am lacking in 79 *Penelope* faithful wife of Ulysses, who put off suitors by weaving 82 *sensible* capable of sensation; *leave* stop

prevailing and to make it brief wars. This is true, on
mine honor; and so, I pray, go with us.

VIRGILIA Give me excuse, good madam. I will obey you 99
in everything hereafter.

VOLUMNIA Let her alone, lady. As she is now, she will
but disease our better mirth.   102

VALERIA In troth, I think she would. Fare you well, then.
Come, good sweet lady. Prithee, Virgilia, turn thy
solemnness out o' door and go along with us.

VIRGILIA No, at a word, madam. Indeed, I must not. I
wish you much mirth.

VALERIA Well, then, farewell.   *Exeunt.*

                              *

Enter Marcius, Titus Lartius, with Drum and   I, iv
Colors, with Captains and Soldiers, as before the city
Corioles. To them a Messenger.

MARCIUS
Yonder comes news. A wager they have met.

LARTIUS
My horse to yours, no.

MARCIUS   'Tis done.

LARTIUS   Agreed.

MARCIUS
Say, has our general met the enemy?

MESSENGER
They lie in view, but have not spoke as yet.   4

LARTIUS
So, the good horse is mine.

MARCIUS   I'll buy him of you.

LARTIUS
No, I'll nor sell nor give him. Lend you him I will
For half a hundred years. Summon the town.

99 *Give me excuse* excuse me 102 *disease* make uneasy; *better mirth*
enjoyment which will be greater without her
I, iv Before the gates of Corioli 4 *spoke* encountered

MARCIUS

How far off lie these armies?

MESSENGER   Within this mile and half.

MARCIUS

9   Then shall we hear their 'larum, and they ours.

Now, Mars, I prithee, make us quick in work,

That we with smoking swords may march from hence,

12   To help our fielded friends! Come, blow thy blast.

> *They sound a parley.*
> *Enter two Senators, with others, on the walls of*
> *Corioles.*

Tullus Aufidius, is he within your walls?

FIRST SENATOR

No, nor a man that fears you less than he:

15   That's lesser than a little.

> *Drum afar off.*   Hark! our drums

Are bringing forth our youth. We'll break our walls

17   Rather than they shall pound us up. Our gates,

Which yet seem shut, we have but pinned with rushes;

They'll open of themselves.

> *Alarum afar off.*   Hark you, far off!

There is Aufidius. List what work he makes

21   Amongst your cloven army.

MARCIUS   O, they are at it!

LARTIUS

22   Their noise be our instruction. Ladders, ho!

> *Enter the army of the Volsces.*

MARCIUS

They fear us not, but issue forth their city.

Now put your shields before your hearts, and fight

25   With hearts more proof than shields. Advance, brave
       Titus.

They do disdain us much beyond our thoughts,

---

9 *'larum* call to arms   12 *fielded* in the battlefield   15 *lesser than a little* next
to nothing   17 *pound* pen   21 *cloven* split   22 *our instruction* a lesson to us
25 *proof* impenetrable

Which makes me sweat with wrath. Come on, my
  fellows.
He that retires, I'll take him for a Volsce,
And he shall feel mine edge.   29
    Alarum. The Romans are beat back to their trenches.
    Enter Marcius, cursing.

MARCIUS
All the contagion of the south light on you,
You shames of Rome! you herd of – Boils and plagues
Plaster you o'er, that you may be abhorred
Farther than seen, and one infect another
Against the wind a mile! You souls of geese,
That bear the shapes of men, how have you run
From slaves that apes would beat! Pluto and hell!
All hurt behind! backs red, and faces pale
With flight and agued fear! Mend and charge home,   38
Or, by the fires of heaven, I'll leave the foe
And make my wars on you! Look to't. Come on!
If you'll stand fast, we'll beat them to their wives,
As they us to our trenches. Follow me!
    Another alarum and Marcius follows them to gates
    and is shut in.
So, now the gates are ope. Now prove good seconds.   43
'Tis for the followers fortune widens them,   44
Not for the fliers. Mark me, and do the like.   45
    Enter the gates.

FIRST SOLDIER
Foolhardiness, not I.
SECOND SOLDIER   Nor I.
FIRST SOLDIER
See, they have shut him in.
    Alarum continues.
ALL   To th' pot, I warrant him.   47

---

29 *edge* sword   **38** *agued* trembling; *home* to the utmost   **43** *ope* open;
seconds supporters   **44** *followers* pursuers   **45** *fliers* pursued   **47** *To th' pot*
to destruction

Enter Titus Lartius.

LARTIUS
What is become of Marcius?

ALL   Slain, sir, doubtless.

FIRST SOLDIER
Following the fliers at the very heels,
With them he enters, who upon the sudden
Clapped to their gates; he is himself alone,
To answer all the city.

LARTIUS   O noble fellow!
53 Who sensibly outdares his senseless sword,
And, when it bows, stand'st up. Thou art left, Marcius.
A carbuncle entire, as big as thou art,
Were not so rich a jewel. Thou wast a soldier
57 Even to Cato's wish, not fierce and terrible
Only in strokes; but with thy grim looks and
The thunder-like percussion of thy sounds,
Thou mad'st thine enemies shake, as if the world
61 Were feverous and did tremble.

Enter Marcius, bleeding, assaulted by the Enemy.

FIRST SOLDIER   Look, sir.

LARTIUS   O, 'tis Marcius!
62 Let's fetch him off, or make remain alike.

They fight, and all enter the City.

*

I, v   *Enter certain Romans, with spoils.*

FIRST ROMAN This will I carry to Rome.

SECOND ROMAN And I this.

3 THIRD ROMAN A murrain on't! I took this for silver.

Alarum continues still afar off.
Enter Marcius and Titus Lartius, with a Trumpet.

---

53 *sensibly* feelingly; *senseless* insensate   57 *Cato* the Censor, exponent of
Roman ethics   61 *feverous* feverish   62 *make remain alike* stay there
similarly
I, v A street in Corioli   3 *murrain* cattle plague; s.d. *Trumpet* trumpeter

MARCIUS
  See here these movers that do prize their hours   4
  At a cracked drachma! Cushions, leaden spoons,   5
  Irons of a doit, doublets that hangmen would   6
  Bury with those that wore them, these base slaves,
  Ere yet the fight be done, pack up. Down with them!
  And hark, what noise the general makes! To him!
  There is the man of my soul's hate, Aufidius,
  Piercing our Romans. Then, valiant Titus, take
  Convenient numbers to make good the city;
  Whilst I, with those that have the spirit, will haste
  To help Cominius.
LARTIUS   Worthy sir, thou bleed'st.
  Thy exercise hath been too violent
  For a second course of fight.   16
MARCIUS   Sir, praise me not.
  My work hath yet not warmed me. Fare you well.
  The blood I drop is rather physical   18
  Than dangerous to me. To Aufidius thus
  I will appear and fight.
LARTIUS   Now the fair goddess Fortune
  Fall deep in love with thee, and her great charms
  Misguide thy opposers' swords! Bold gentleman,
  Prosperity be thy page!
MARCIUS   Thy friend no less
  Than those she placeth highest. So, farewell.   24
LARTIUS
  Thou worthiest Marcius!   [Exit Marcius.]
  Go sound thy trumpet in the market-place.
  Call thither all the officers o' th' town,
  Where they shall know our mind. Away!   Exeunt.

*

4 *movers* active men; *prize their hours* value their time   5 *drachma* Greek
coin   6 *of a doit* worth the smallest sum; *hangmen* (whose perquisites
included the clothes of the hanged)   16 *course* round; *praise* appraise
18 *physical* curative   24 *those* friend to those

I, vi   *Enter Cominius, as it were in retire, with Soldiers.*

COMINIUS

Breathe you, my friends. Well fought ! We are come off
Like Romans, neither foolish in our stands
3   Nor cowardly in retire. Believe me, sirs,
We shall be charged again. Whiles we have struck,
5   By interims and conveying gusts we have heard
The charges of our friends. The Roman gods
7   Lead their successes as we wish our own,
That both our powers, with smiling fronts encount'ring,
May give you thankful sacrifice.
          Enter a Messenger.   Thy news ?

MESSENGER

10   The citizens of Corioles have issued,
And given to Lartius and to Marcius battle.
I saw our party to their trenches driven,
And then I came away.

COMINIUS   Though thou speakest truth,
Methinks thou speak'st not well. How long is't since ?

MESSENGER

Above an hour, my lord.

COMINIUS

16   'Tis not a mile ; briefly we heard their drums.
17   How couldst thou in a mile confound an hour,
And bring thy news so late ?

MESSENGER   Spies of the Volsces
19   Held me in chase, that I was forced to wheel
Three or four miles about ; else had I, sir,
Half an hour since brought my report.

COMINIUS   Who's yonder,
That does appear as he were flayed ? O gods !
He has the stamp of Marcius, and I have
24   Beforetime seen him thus.

I, vi An open place near the Roman camp   3 *retire* withdrawal   5 *conveying*
carrying the noise of battle   7 *successes* fortunes   10 *issued* sallied forth
16 *briefly* a short while ago   17 *confound* waste   19 *that* so that   24
Beforetime in former time

Enter Marcius.

MARCIUS   Come I too late ?

COMINIUS

The shepherd knows not thunder from a tabor   25
More than I know the sound of Marcius' tongue
From every meaner man.

MARCIUS   Come I too late ?

COMINIUS

Ay, if you come not in the blood of others,
But mantled in your own.

MARCIUS   O, let me clip ye   29
In arms as sound as when I wooed, in heart
As merry as when our nuptial day was done,
And tapers burned to bedward !   32

COMINIUS   Flower of warriors !
How is't with Titus Lartius ?

MARCIUS

As with a man busied about decrees :
Condemning some to death, and some to exile ;
Ransoming him or pitying, threatening th' other ;   36
Holding Corioles in the name of Rome,
Even like a fawning greyhound in the leash,
To let him slip at will.   39

COMINIUS   Where is that slave
Which told me they had beat you to your trenches ?
Where is he ? Call him hither.

MARCIUS   Let him alone.
He did inform the truth. But for our gentlemen,
The common file, – a plague ! tribunes for them ! –   43
The mouse ne'er shunned the cat as they did budge
From rascals worse than they.

COMINIUS   But how prevailed you ?

MARCIUS

Will the time serve to tell ? I do not think.

25 *tabor* small drum   29 *clip* embrace   32 *tapers burned to bedward* candles indicated bedtime   36 *Ransoming* releasing   39 *let him slip* unleash him 43 *common file* rank and file

Where is the enemy ? Are you lords o' th' field ?
If not, why cease you till you are so ?

COMINIUS   Marcius,
We have at disadvantage fought and did
Retire to win our purpose.

MARCIUS
How lies their battle ? Know you on which side
They have placed their men of trust ?

COMINIUS   As I guess, Marcius,
53 Their bands i' th' vaward are the Antiates,
Of their best trust ; o'er them Aufidius,
Their very heart of hope.

MARCIUS   I do beseech you
By all the battles wherein we have fought,
By th' blood we have shed together, by th' vows
58 We have made to endure friends, that you directly
Set me against Aufidius and his Antiates ;
And that you not delay the present, but,
Filling the air with swords advanced and darts,
62 We prove this very hour.

COMINIUS   Though I could wish
You were conducted to a gentle bath
And balms applied to you, yet dare I never
Deny your asking. Take your choice of those
That best can aid your action.

MARCIUS   Those are they
That most are willing. If any such be here –
As it were sin to doubt – that love this painting
69 Wherein you see me smeared ; if any fear
Lesser his person than an ill report ;
If any think brave death outweighs bad life,
And that his country 's dearer than himself ;
Let him alone, or so many so minded,
Wave thus, to express his disposition,
And follow Marcius.

53 *vaward* vanguard   58 *endure* remain   62 *prove* test   69–70 *fear Lesser*
fear less for

50

*They all shout and wave their swords, take him up in
their arms, and cast up their caps.*

O, me alone! Make you a sword of me?
If these shows be not outward, which of you   77
But is four Volsces? None of you but is
Able to bear against the great Aufidius
A shield as hard as his. A certain number,
Though thanks to all, must I select. The rest
Shall bear the business in some other fight,
As cause will be obeyed. Please you to march;   83
And four shall quickly draw out my command,
Which men are best inclined.
COMINIUS   March on, my fellows.
Make good this ostentation, and you shall   86
Divide in all with us.   *Exeunt.*

                    *

Titus Lartius, having set a guard upon Corioles,   I, vii
going with Drum and Trumpet toward Cominius and
Caius Marcius, enters with a Lieutenant, other
Soldiers, and a Scout.

LARTIUS
So, let the ports be guarded. Keep your duties,   1
As I have set them down. If I do send, dispatch
Those centuries to our aid; the rest will serve   3
For a short holding. If we lose the field,
We cannot keep the town.
LIEUTENANT   Fear not our care, sir.   5
LARTIUS
Hence, and shut your gates upon's.
Our guider, come; to th' Roman camp conduct us.   7
                                          Exeunt.

                    *

77 *shows* gestures   83 *cause will be obeyed* circumstances require   86
ostentation showing
I, vii Before the gates of Corioli   1 *ports* gates   3 *centuries* companies of a
hundred   5 *Fear not* do not worry about   7 *guider* guide

51

I, viii   *Alarum, as in battle. Enter Marcius and Aufidius at
several doors.*

MARCIUS

I'll fight with none but thee, for I do hate thee
Worse than a promise-breaker.

AUFIDIUS   We hate alike.
3   Not Afric owns a serpent I abhor
4   More than thy fame and envy. Fix thy foot.

MARCIUS

Let the first budger die the other's slave,
And the gods doom him after!

AUFIDIUS   If I fly, Marcius,
7   Hollo me like a hare.

MARCIUS   Within these three hours, Tullus,
Alone I fought in your Corioles walls,
And made what work I pleased. 'Tis not my blood
Wherein thou seest me masked. For thy revenge
Wrench up thy power to th' highest.

AUFIDIUS   Wert thou the Hector
12   That was the whip of your bragged progeny,
13   Thou shouldst not scape me here.

       *Here they fight, and certain Volsces come in the aid of
Aufidius. Marcius fights till they be driven in
breathless.*

14   Officious and not valiant, you have shamed me
15   In your condemnèd seconds.   *[Exeunt.]*

I, ix   *Flourish. Alarum. A retreat is sounded. Flourish.
Enter, at one door, Cominius, with the Romans; at
another door, Marcius, with his arm in a scarf.*

COMINIUS

If I should tell thee o'er this thy day's work,
2   Thou't not believe thy deeds. But I'll report it

I, viii An open place near the Roman camp   s.d. *at several doors* from
different entrances   3 *Afric* Africa   4 *fame and envy* enviable fame   7
Hollo hunt down   12 *whip* champion; *bragged progeny* boasted progenitors
13 *scape* escape   14 *Officious* meddling   15 *condemnèd seconds* ineffectual aid
I, ix   2 *Thou't* thou wouldst

Where senators shall mingle tears with smiles;
Where great patricians shall attend and shrug,
I' th' end admire; where ladies shall be frighted,
And, gladly quaked, hear more; where the dull tribunes, 6
That with the fusty plebeians hate thine honors, 7
Shall say against their hearts, 'We thank the gods
Our Rome hath such a soldier.'
Yet camest thou to a morsel of this feast, 10
Having fully dined before.
    *Enter Titus [Lartius], with his Power, from the
    pursuit.*
LARTIUS   O general,
Here is the steed, we the caparison. 12
Hadst thou beheld –
MARCIUS   Pray now, no more. My mother,
Who has a charter to extol her blood, 14
When she does praise me grieves me. I have done
As you have done – that's what I can; induced
As you have been – that's for my country.
He that has but effected his good will 18
Hath overta'en mine act.
COMINIUS   You shall not be 19
The grave of your deserving. Rome must know
The value of her own. 'Twere a concealment
Worse than a theft, no less than a traducement, 22
To hide your doings and to silence that
Which, to the spire and top of praises vouched, 24
Would seem but modest. Therefore, I beseech you – 25
In sign of what you are, not to reward 26
What you have done – before our army hear me.
MARCIUS
I have some wounds upon me, and they smart

---

6 *quaked* made to tremble   **7** *fusty* mouldy; *plebeians* lowest class   **10** *of* in
12 *caparison* trappings   **14** *charter* privilege   **18** *effected his good will*
accomplished his intention   **19–20** *You . . . deserving* you shall not bury
your merit   **22** *traducement* slander   **24** *vouched* attested   **25** *modest*
moderate   **26** *sign* token

To hear themselves rememb'red.

COMINIUS   Should they not,
30   Well might they fester 'gainst ingratitude
31   And tent themselves with death. Of all the horses,
32   Whereof we have ta'en good and good store, of all
The treasure in this field achieved and city,
We render you the tenth, to be ta'en forth
Before the common distribution at
Your only choice.

MARCIUS   I thank you, general,
But cannot make my heart consent to take
A bribe to pay my sword. I do refuse it,
And stand upon my common part with those
That have beheld the doing.

> *A long flourish. They all cry, 'Marcius! Marcius!',
> cast up their caps and lances. Cominius and Lartius
> stand bare.*

MARCIUS

May these same instruments which you profane
Never sound more! When drums and trumpets shall
I' th' field prove flatterers, let courts and cities be
44   Made all of false-faced soothing! When steel grows
45   Soft as the parasite's silk, let him be made
46   A coverture for th' wars. No more, I say!
For that I have not washed my nose that bled,
48   Or foiled some debile wretch, which without note
Here's many else have done, you shout me forth
In acclamations hyperbolical,
51   As if I loved my little should be dieted
In praises sauced with lies.

COMINIUS   Too modest are you,
More cruel to your good report than grateful

---

30 *'gainst* exposed to   **31** *tent* cure by probing   **32** *good and good store*
good in quality and quantity   **44** *false-faced soothing* hypocritical flattery
45 *him* i.e. the silk   **46** *coverture* covering   **48** *foiled* have defeated; *debile*
weak; *without note* unnoticed   **51** *little* small share; *dieted* fed

To us that give you truly. By your patience,   54
If 'gainst yourself you be incensed, we'll put you,
Like one that means his proper harm, in manacles,   56
Then reason safely with you. Therefore be it known,
As to us, to all the world, that Caius Marcius
Wears this war's garland; in token of the which,
My noble steed, known to the camp, I give him,
With all his trim belonging; and from this time,   61
For what he did before Corioles, call him,
With all th' applause and clamor of the host,
Caius Marcius Coriolanus. Bear
Th' addition nobly ever!   65
    Flourish. Trumpets sound, and drums.

ALL
Caius Marcius Coriolanus!
CORIOLANUS
I will go wash;
And when my face is fair, you shall perceive
Whether I blush or no. Howbeit, I thank you.
I mean to stride your steed, and at all times
To undercrest your good addition   71
To th' fairness of my power.   72
COMINIUS   So, to our tent,
Where, ere we do repose us, we will write
To Rome of our success. You, Titus Lartius,
Must to Corioles back. Send us to Rome
The best, with whom we may articulate,   76
For their own good and ours.
LARTIUS   I shall, my lord.
CORIOLANUS
The gods begin to mock me. I, that now
Refused most princely gifts, am bound to beg
Of my lord general.

---

54 *give* represent **56** *means* intends; *proper* own **61** *trim belonging* apper-
taining equipment **65** *addition* title **71** *undercrest* adopt and justify
(heraldic) **72** *To . . . power* as fairly as I can **76** *articulate* come to terms

COMINIUS   Take't, 'tis yours. What is't?
CORIOLANUS
81   I sometime lay here in Corioles
82   At a poor man's house; he used me kindly.
83   He cried to me; I saw him prisoner;
      But then Aufidius was within my view,
      And wrath o'erwhelmed my pity. I request you
      To give my poor host freedom.
COMINIUS   O, well begged!
      Were he the butcher of my son, he should
      Be free as is the wind. Deliver him, Titus.
LARTIUS
      Marcius, his name?
CORIOLANUS   By Jupiter, forgot!
      I am weary; yea, my memory is tired.
      Have we no wine here?
COMINIUS   Go we to our tent.
      The blood upon your visage dries; 'tis time
      It should be looked to. Come.   *Exeunt.*

*

I, x   *A flourish. Cornets. Enter Tullus Aufidius, bloody,*
              with two or three Soldiers.
AUFIDIUS
      The town is ta'en.
FIRST SOLDIER
2   'Twill be delivered back on good condition.
AUFIDIUS
      Condition?
      I would I were a Roman; for I cannot,
      Being a Volsce, be that I am. Condition?
      What good condition can a treaty find
7   I' th' part that is at mercy? Five times, Marcius,

81 *sometime lay* once lodged   82 *used* treated   83 *cried* cried out
I, x The camp of the Volsces   2 *good condition* favorable terms   7 *I' th' part*
for the side; *at mercy* in the victor's power

56

I have fought with thee ; so often hast thou beat me,
And wouldst do so, I think, should we encounter
As often as we eat. By th' elements,
If e'er again I meet him beard to beard,
He's mine or I am his. Mine emulation   12
Hath not that honor in't it had ; for where
I thought to crush him in an equal force,
True sword to sword, I'll potch at him some way ;   15
Or wrath or craft may get him.

FIRST SOLDIER   He's the devil.

AUFIDIUS
Bolder, though not so subtle. My valor 's poisoned
With only suffering stain by him ; for him
Shall fly out of itself. Nor sleep nor sanctuary,   19
Being naked, sick, nor fane nor capitol,   20
The prayers of priests nor times of sacrifice,
Embargements all of fury, shall lift up   22
Their rotten privilege and custom 'gainst
My hate to Marcius. Where I find him, were it
At home, upon my brother's guard, even there,   25
Against the hospitable canon, would I   26
Wash my fierce hand in's heart. Go you to th' city.
Learn how 'tis held, and what they are that must
Be hostages for Rome.

FIRST SOLDIER   Will not you go ?

AUFIDIUS
I am attended at the cypress grove : I pray you –
'Tis south the city mills – bring me word thither
How the world goes, that to the pace of it
I may spur on my journey.

FIRST SOLDIER   I shall, sir.   [Exeunt.]

                              *

12 *emulation* rivalry   15 *potch* make a stab   19 *Shall . . . itself* it shall
deviate from its nature   20 *fane* shrine   22 *Embargements* restraints   25
upon under   26 *hospitable canon* law of hospitality

II, i   *Enter Menenius, with the two Tribunes of the People,*
        Sicinius and Brutus.

1 MENENIUS The augurer tells me we shall have news to-
night.

BRUTUS Good or bad?

MENENIUS Not according to the prayer of the people, for
they love not Marcius.

SICINIUS Nature teaches beasts to know their friends.

MENENIUS Pray you, who does the wolf love?

SICINIUS The lamb.

MENENIUS Ay, to devour him, as the hungry plebeians
would the noble Marcius.

BRUTUS He's a lamb indeed, that baas like a bear.

MENENIUS He's a bear indeed, that lives like a lamb. You
two are old men: tell me one thing that I shall ask you.

BOTH Well, sir.

14 MENENIUS In what enormity is Marcius poor in, that you
two have not in abundance?

BRUTUS He's poor in no one fault, but stored with all.

SICINIUS Especially in pride.

BRUTUS And topping all others in boasting.

MENENIUS This is strange now. Do you two know how
20   you are censured here in the city, I mean of us o' th'
21   right-hand file? Do you?

BOTH Why, how are we censured?

MENENIUS Because you talk of pride now – will you not
be angry?

BOTH Well, well, sir, well.

26 MENENIUS Why, 'tis no great matter; for a very little
thief of occasion will rob you of a great deal of patience.
Give your dispositions the reins and be angry at your
pleasures – at the least, if you take it as a pleasure to you
in being so. You blame Marcius for being proud?

II, i A public place in Rome   1 *augurer* soothsayer   14 *enormity* vice   20
censured judged   21 *right-hand file* ruling class   26–27 *a very . . . patience*
you get very impatient upon the slightest pretext

BRUTUS We do it not alone, sir.

MENENIUS I know you can do very little alone; for your
  helps are many, or else your actions would grow won-   33
  drous single. Your abilities are too infant-like for doing
  much alone. You talk of pride: O that you could turn
  your eyes toward the napes of your necks, and make but
  an interior survey of your good selves! O that you could!

BRUTUS What then, sir?

MENENIUS Why, then you should discover a brace of un-
  meriting, proud, violent, testy magistrates, alias fools,
  as any in Rome.

SICINIUS Menenius, you are known well enough too.

MENENIUS I am known to be a humorous patrician, and   43
  one that loves a cup of hot wine with not a drop of allay-   44
  ing Tiber in't; said to be something imperfect in favor-   45
  ing the first complaint; hasty and tinder-like upon too
  trivial motion; one that converses more with the buttock   47
  of the night than with the forehead of the morning.
  What I think, I utter, and spend my malice in my
  breath. Meeting two such wealsmen as you are, – I can-   50
  not call you Lycurguses – if the drink you give me touch   51
  my palate adversely, I make a crooked face at it. I cannot
  say your worships have delivered the matter well, when
  I find the ass in compound with the major part of your   54
  syllables; and though I must be content to bear with
  those that say you are reverend grave men, yet they lie
  deadly that tell you you have good faces. If you see this
  in the map of my microcosm, follows it that I am known   58
  well enough too? What harm can your bisson conspec-   59
  tuities glean out of this character, if I be known well
  enough too?

33–34 *wondrous single* extraordinarily feeble   43 *humorous* whimsical
44–45 *allaying Tiber* diluting river-water   45–46 *imperfect . . . complaint*
prone to sympathize   47 *motion* motive   47–48 *one . . . morning* more used
to staying up late than rising early   50 *wealsmen* statesmen   51 *Lycurgus*
Spartan lawgiver   54 *ass in compound* phrases beginning 'whereas'   58 *map*
face; *microcosm* body   59 *bisson conspectuities* blinded eyesights

BRUTUS Come, sir, come, we know you well enough.

MENENIUS You know neither me, yourselves, nor any-
63 thing. You are ambitious for poor knaves' caps and legs.
You wear out a good wholesome forenoon in hearing a
65 cause between an orange-wife and a forset-seller, and
66 then rejourn the controversy of threepence to a second
day of audience. When you are hearing a matter between party and party, if you chance to be pinched with
69 the colic, you make faces like mummers; set up the
bloody flag against all patience; and, in roaring for a
71 chamber-pot, dismiss the controversy bleeding, the
more entangled by your hearing. All the peace you
make in their cause is, calling both the parties knaves.
You are a pair of strange ones.

74 BRUTUS Come, come, you are well understood to be a
perfecter giber for the table than a necessary bencher in
the Capitol.

MENENIUS Our very priests must become mockers, if
they shall encounter such ridiculous subjects as you are.
When you speak best unto the purpose, it is not worth
the wagging of your beards; and your beards deserve
81 not so honorable a grave as to stuff a botcher's cushion
or to be entombed in an ass's pack-saddle. Yet you
must be saying Marcius is proud; who, in a cheap esti-
84 mation, is worth all your predecessors since Deucalion,
though peradventure some of the best of 'em were
hereditary hangmen. Good-e'en to your worships.
87 More of your conversation would infect my brain, being
the herdsmen of the beastly plebeians. I will be bold to
take my leave of you.

Brutus and Sicinius aside.

63 *caps* doffing of hats; *legs* bows   65 *orange-wife* street-vendor; *forset*
wine-tap   66 *rejourn* postpone   69 *mummers* masqueraders   69–70 *set ...
against* declare war on   71 *bleeding* unhealed   74–76 *a perfecter ... Capitol*
rather a dinner-table wit than a serious judge   81 *botcher* clothes-mender
84 *Deucalion* survivor of the Flood   87 *being* since you are

Enter Volumnia, Virgilia, and Valeria.

How now, my as fair as noble ladies, – and the moon,
were she earthly, no nobler – whither do you follow
your eyes so fast?

VOLUMNIA Honorable Menenius, my boy Marcius approaches. For the love of Juno, let's go.

MENENIUS Ha? Marcius coming home?

VOLUMNIA Ay, worthy Menenius, and with most pros-
perous approbation.

MENENIUS Take my cap, Jupiter, and I thank thee. Hoo!   97
Marcius coming home!

TWO LADIES Nay, 'tis true.

VOLUMNIA Look, here's a letter from him. The state hath
another, his wife another; and, I think, there's one at
home for you.

MENENIUS I will make my very house reel to-night. A
letter for me!

VIRGILIA Yes, certain, there's a letter for you; I saw't.

MENENIUS A letter for me! It gives me an estate of seven
years' health, in which time I will make a lip at the   107
physician. The most sovereign prescription in Galen is   108
but empiricutic and, to this preservative, of no better   109
report than a horse-drench. Is he not wounded? He   110
was wont to come home wounded.

VIRGILIA O, no, no, no.

VOLUMNIA O, he is wounded; I thank the gods for't.

MENENIUS So do I too, if it be not too much. Brings 'a   114
victory in his pocket? The wounds become him.

VOLUMNIA On's brows. Menenius, he comes the third
time home with the oaken garland.

MENENIUS Has he disciplined Aufidius soundly?

VOLUMNIA Titus Lartius writes they fought together,
but Aufidius got off.

---

97 *Take . . . Jupiter* I throw my cap in the air   107 *make a lip at* mock
108 *sovereign* efficacious; *Galen* Greek medical authority   109 *empiricutic*
quackish; *to* compared to   110 *drench* dose   114 *'a* he (familiar)

MENENIUS And 'twas time for him too, I'll warrant him
that. An he had stayed by him, I would not have been so
123   fidiused for all the chests in Corioles and the gold that's
124   in them. Is the Senate possessed of this?

VOLUMNIA Good ladies, let's go. Yes, yes, yes! The
Senate has letters from the general, wherein he gives my
127   son the whole name of the war. He hath in this action
outdone his former deeds doubly.

129   VALERIA In troth, there's wondrous things spoke of him.

MENENIUS Wondrous? Ay, I warrant you, and not with-
131   out his true purchasing.

VIRGILIA The gods grant them true!

133   VOLUMNIA True? pow waw!

MENENIUS True? I'll be sworn they are true. Where is he
wounded? *[to the Tribunes]* God save your good worships! Marcius is coming home. He has more cause to be
proud. – Where is he wounded?

VOLUMNIA I' th' shoulder and i' th' left arm. There will be
139   large cicatrices to show the people, when he shall stand
140   for his place. He received in the repulse of Tarquin
seven hurts i' th' body.

MENENIUS One i' th' neck and two i' th' thigh – there's
nine that I know.

VOLUMNIA He had, before this last expedition, twenty-
five wounds upon him.

MENENIUS Now it's twenty-seven. Every gash was an
enemy's grave. *(A shout and flourish.)* Hark! the
trumpets.

VOLUMNIA These are the ushers of Marcius. Before him
he carries noise, and behind him he leaves tears.
150   Death, that dark spirit, in's nervy arm doth lie;
151   Which, being advanced, declines, and then men die.

---

123 *fidiused* treated like Aufidius   124 *possessed* fully informed   127 *name*
credit   129 *troth* truth   131 *purchasing* winning   133 *pow waw* pooh
139 *cicatrices* scars; *stand* be a candidate   140 *Tarquin* deposed Roman
tyrant   150 *nervy* sinewy   151 *declines* sinks down

A sennet. Trumpets sound. Enter Cominius the
General and Titus Lartius ; between them,
Coriolanus, crowned with an oaken garland ; with
Captains and Soldiers and a Herald.

HERALD
Know, Rome, that all alone Marcius did fight
Within Corioles gates, where he hath won,
With fame, a name to Caius Marcius. These   154
In honor follows Coriolanus.
Welcome to Rome, renownèd Coriolanus!
    Sound. Flourish.

ALL
Welcome to Rome, renownèd Coriolanus!

CORIOLANUS
No more of this; it does offend my heart.
Pray now, no more.

COMINIUS   Look, sir, your mother!

CORIOLANUS   O,
You have, I know, petitioned all the gods
For my prosperity!
    Kneels.

VOLUMNIA   Nay, my good soldier, up.
My gentle Marcius, worthy Caius, and
By deed-achieving honor newly named –   163
What is it ? – Coriolanus must I call thee ? –
But, O, thy wife!

CORIOLANUS   My gracious silence, hail!
Wouldst thou have laughed had I come coffined home,
That weep'st to see me triumph? Ah, my dear,
Such eyes the widows in Corioles wear,
And mothers that lack sons.

MENENIUS   Now, the gods crown thee!

CORIOLANUS
And live you yet ? *[to Valeria]* O my sweet lady, pardon.

---

151 s.d. *sennet* trumpet signal   **154** *With* along with; *to* in addition to   **163**
deed-achieving achieved by deeds

VOLUMNIA
  I know not where to turn. O, welcome home!
  And welcome, General! and y' are welcome all!

MENENIUS
  A hundred thousand welcomes! I could weep
174 And I could laugh; I am light and heavy. Welcome.
175 A curse begin at very root on's heart
  That is not glad to see thee! You are three
  That Rome should dote on; yet, by the faith of men,
  We have some old crab-trees here at home that will not
179 Be grafted to your relish. Yet welcome, warriors!
  We call a nettle but a nettle and
  The faults of fools but folly.

COMINIUS   Ever right.

CORIOLANUS
182 Menenius, ever, ever.

HERALD
  Give way there, and go on!

CORIOLANUS *[to Volumnia and Virgilia]*
                Your hand, and yours.
  Ere in our own house I do shade my head,
  The good patricians must be visited;
  From whom I have received not only greetings,
187 But with them change of honors.

VOLUMNIA   I have lived
188 To see inherited my very wishes
  And the buildings of my fancy. Only
  There's one thing wanting, which I doubt not but
  Our Rome will cast upon thee.

CORIOLANUS   Know, good mother,
  I had rather be their servant in my way,
193 Than sway with them in theirs.

174 *light* joyful; *heavy* sad   175 *begin at* penetrate to; *on's* of his   179
grafted to your relish implanted with a liking for you   182 *ever* still the same
187 *change of honors* promotion   188 *inherited* realized   193 *sway* rule

COMINIUS   On, to the Capitol!
    Flourish. Cornets. Exeunt in state, as before. Brutus
    and Sicinius [come forward].

BRUTUS
  All tongues speak of him, and the bleared sights   194
  Are spectacled to see him. Your prattling nurse
  Into a rapture lets her baby cry,   196
  While she chats him; the kitchen malkin pins   197
  Her richest lockram 'bout her reechy neck,   198
  Clamb'ring the walls to eye him. Stalls, bulks, windows   199
  Are smothered up, leads filled, and ridges horsed   200
  With variable complexions, all agreeing   201
  In earnestness to see him. Seld-shown flamens   202
  Do press among the popular throngs, and puff
  To win a vulgar station. Our veiled dames   204
  Commit the war of white and damask in   205
  Their nicely-gawded cheeks to th' wanton spoil   206
  Of Phoebus' burning kisses – such a pother   207
  As if that whatsoever god who leads him
  Were slily crept into his human powers
  And gave him graceful posture.
SICINIUS   On the sudden,
  I warrant him consul.   211
BRUTUS   Then our office may,
  During his power, go sleep.
SICINIUS
  He cannot temp'rately transport his honors
  From where he should begin and end, but will   214
  Lose those he hath won.
BRUTUS   In that there's comfort.
SICINIUS   Doubt not

194 *sights* eyesights   196 *rapture* fit   197 *chats* gossips about; *malkin*
slattern   198 *lockram* coarse linen; *reechy* grimy   199 *bulks* shop-fronts
200 *leads* leaden roofs; *ridges horsed* roof-tops bestridden   201 *variable
complexions* different types   202 *Seld-shown flamens* priests who rarely
appear   204 *vulgar station* place in the crowd   205 *damask* red   206 *nicely-
gawded* daintily adorned   207 *Phoebus* the sun; *pother* turmoil   211 *consul*
one of Rome's two chief magistrats   214 *and end* to where he should end

The commoners, for whom we stand, but they
217   Upon their ancient malice will forget
With the least cause these his new honors, which
That he will give them make I as little question
220   As he is proud to do't.

BRUTUS   I heard him swear,
Were he to stand for consul, never would he
Appear i' th' market-place nor on him put
223   The napless vesture of humility;
Nor, showing, as the manner is, his wounds
To th' people, beg their stinking breaths.

SICINIUS   'Tis right.

BRUTUS
It was his word: O, he would miss it rather
227   Than carry it but by the suit of the gentry to him
And the desire of the nobles.

SICINIUS   I wish no better
Than have him hold that purpose and to put it
In execution.

230   BRUTUS   'Tis most like he will.

SICINIUS
231   It shall be to him then as our good wills,
A sure destruction.

BRUTUS   So it must fall out
To him or our authorities for an end.
234   We must suggest the people in what hatred
He still hath held them; that to's power he would
Have made them mules, silenced their pleaders, and
237   Dispropertied their freedoms, holding them,
In human action and capacity,
Of no more soul nor fitness for the world
240   Than camels in their war, who have their provand
241   Only for bearing burthens, and sore blows

---

217 *Upon . . . malice* because of their longstanding hostility   220 *As* as that
223 *napless* threadbare   227 *carry* win   230 *like* likely   231 *good wills*
advantage requires   234 *suggest* insinuate to   237 *Dispropertied* dis-
possessed   240 *provand* provender   241 *burthens* burdens

For sinking under them.
SICINIUS   This, as you say, suggested
At some time when his soaring insolence
Shall touch the people – which time shall not want,   244
If he be put upon't, and that's as easy   245
As to set dogs on sheep – will be his fire
To kindle their dry stubble ; and their blaze
Shall darken him for ever.
          Enter a Messenger.
BRUTUS   What's the matter ?
MESSENGER
You are sent for to th' Capitol. 'Tis thought
That Marcius shall be consul.
I have seen the dumb men throng to see him, and
The blind to hear him speak. Matrons flung gloves,
Ladies and maids their scarfs and handkerchers,
Upon him as he passed. The nobles bended,
As to Jove's statue, and the commons made
A shower and thunder with their caps and shouts.
I never saw the like.
BRUTUS   Let's to the Capitol,
And carry with us ears and eyes for th' time,   258
But hearts for the event.   259
SICINIUS   Have with you.   *Exeunt.*

*

          Enter two Officers, to lay cushions, as it were in the   II, ii
          Capitol.
FIRST OFFICER Come, come, they are almost here. How
many stand for consulships ?
SECOND OFFICER Three, they say ; but 'tis thought of 3
every one Coriolanus will carry it.

---

244 *which . . . want* and that time will come   245 *put upon't* provoked
258 *time* situation   259 *event* outcome
II, ii The Roman senate house in the Capitol   s.d. *cushions* used on stage
for seats   3 *of* by

5 FIRST OFFICER That's a brave fellow; but he's vengeance
proud, and loves not the common people.

SECOND OFFICER Faith, there hath been many great
men that have flattered the people, who ne'er loved
them; and there be many that they have loved, they
know not wherefore; so that, if they love they know not
why, they hate upon no better a ground. Therefore, for
Coriolanus neither to care whether they love or hate
13 him manifests the true knowledge he has in their dis-
14 position, and out of his noble carelessness lets them
plainly see't.

FIRST OFFICER If he did not care whether he had their
16 love or no, he waved indifferently 'twixt doing them
neither good nor harm; but he seeks their hate with
greater devotion than they can render it him, and leaves
19 nothing undone that may fully discover him their
20 opposite. Now to seem to affect the malice and displeasure of the people is as bad as that which he dislikes
– to flatter them for their love.

SECOND OFFICER He hath deserved worthily of his
country; and his ascent is not by such easy degrees as
those who, having been supple and courteous to the
26 people, bonneted, without any further deed to have
them at all into their estimation and report. But he hath
so planted his honors in their eyes and his actions in
their hearts that for their tongues to be silent and not
confess so much were a kind of ingrateful injury; to report otherwise were a malice that, giving itself the lie,
would pluck reproof and rebuke from every ear that
heard it.

FIRST OFFICER No more of him; he's a worthy man.
Make way, they are coming.

---

5 *vengeance* terribly 13 *in* of 14 *carelessness* indifference 16 *waved*
wavered 19–20 *discover . . . opposite* show that he is opposed to them
20 *affect* cultivate 26–27 *bonneted . . . report* did nothing but doff their
hats to attain popularity

A sennet. Enter the Patricians and the Tribunes of 34
the People, Lictors before them : Coriolanus,
Menenius, Cominius the Consul. Sicinius and Brutus
take their places by themselves. Coriolanus stands.

MENENIUS
Having determined of the Volsces and 35
To send for Titus Lartius, it remains,
As the main point of this our after-meeting, 37
To gratify his noble service that 38
Hath thus stood for his country. Therefore, please you,
Most reverend and grave elders, to desire
The present consul, and last general
In our well-found successes, to report 42
A little of that worthy work performed
By Caius Marcius Coriolanus, whom
We met here both to thank and to remember
With honors like himself.

FIRST SENATOR   Speak, good Cominius.
Leave nothing out for length, and make us think
Rather our state's defective for requital 48
Than we to stretch it out. 49
        [*To the Tribunes*]   Masters o' th' people,
We do request your kindest ears, and after,
Your loving motion toward the common body 51
To yield what passes here. 52

SICINIUS   We are convented
Upon a pleasing treaty, and have hearts 53
Inclinable to honor and advance
The theme of our assembly.

BRUTUS   Which the rather 55
We shall be blest to do, if he remember 56

34 s.d. *Lictors* magistrates' attendants   35 *of* concerning   37 *after-meeting* later meeting   38 *gratify* requite   42 *well-found* fortunately encountered   48 *defective for requital* unable to reward adequately   49 *stretch it out* extend it   51 *Your . . . body* your kind mediation with the people   52 *yield* grant; *convented* summoned   53 *Upon* to consider   55 *rather* sooner   56 *blest* happy

A kinder value of the people than
He hath hereto prized them at.

58 MENENIUS   That's off, that's off!
I would you rather had been silent. Please you
To hear Cominius speak?

BRUTUS   Most willingly;
But yet my caution was more pertinent
Than the rebuke you give it.

MENENIUS   He loves your people;
But tie him not to be their bedfellow.
Worthy Cominius, speak.

    Coriolanus rises, and offers to go away.
                Nay, keep your place.

FIRST SENATOR
Sit, Coriolanus. Never shame to hear
What you have nobly done.

CORIOLANUS   Your honors' pardon.
I had rather have my wounds to heal again
Than hear say how I got them.

BRUTUS   Sir, I hope
69 My words disbenched you not.

CORIOLANUS   No, sir. Yet oft,
When blows have made me stay, I fled from words.
71 You soothed not, therefore hurt not: but your people,
I love them as they weigh —

MENENIUS   Pray now, sit down.

CORIOLANUS
73 I had rather have one scratch my head i' th' sun
When the alarum were struck than idly sit
75 To hear my nothings monstered.   *Exit Coriolanus.*

MENENIUS   Masters of the people,
Your multiplying spawn how can he flatter —
That's thousand to one good one — when you now see
He'd rather venture all his limbs for honor

---

58 *off* beside the point   **69** *disbenched you* made you get up   **71** *soothed*
flattered   **73–74** *have . . . struck* be idle during battle   **75** *monstered* made
marvels of

Than one on's ears to hear it? Proceed, Cominius.   79
COMINIUS
  I shall lack voice. The deeds of Coriolanus
  Should not be uttered feebly. It is held
  That valor is the chiefest virtue, and
  Most dignifies the haver. If it be,
  The man I speak of cannot in the world
  Be singly counterpoised. At sixteen years,   85
  When Tarquin made a head for Rome, he fought   86
  Beyond the mark of others. Our then dictator,   87
  Whom with all praise I point at, saw him fight,
  When with his Amazonian chin he drove   89
  The bristled lips before him; he bestrid   90
  An o'erpressed Roman and i' th' consul's view   91
  Slew three opposers; Tarquin's self he met,
  And struck him on his knee. In that day's feats,   93
  When he might act the woman in the scene,
  He proved best man i' th' field, and for his meed
  Was brow-bound with the oak. His pupil age
  Man-entered thus, he waxèd like a sea,   97
  And in the brunt of seventeen battles since
  He lurched all swords of the garland. For this last, 99
  Before and in Corioles, let me say,
  I cannot speak him home. He stopped the fliers,   101
  And by his rare example made the coward
  Turn terror into sport. As weeds before
  A vessel under sail, so men obeyed
  And fell below his stem; his sword, death's stamp,   105
  Where it did mark, it took. From face to foot
  He was a thing of blood, whose every motion
  Was timed with dying cries. Alone he entered   108

---

79 *Than . . . hear it* than venture one of his ears to hear about it   85 *singly counterpoised* equalled by another individual   86 *made . . . for* raised an army to reconquer   87 *dictator* wartime leader   89 *Amazonian* unbearded (like a female warrior)   90 *bestrid* protected   91 *o'erpressed* overwhelmed   93 *on* to   97 *Man-entered* initiated into manhood; *waxèd* grew   99 *lurched* robbed   101 *home* sufficiently   105 *stem* bow   108 *timed* rhythmically accompanied

109   The mortal gate of th' city, which he painted
110   With shunless destiny; aidless came off,
       And with a sudden reinforcement struck
       Corioles like a planet. Now all's his,
113   When by and by the din of war gan pierce
114   His ready sense; then straight his doubled spirit
115   Requickened what in flesh was fatigate,
       And to the battle came he; where he did
117   Run reeking o'er the lives of men, as if
       'Twere a perpetual spoil, and till we called
119   Both field and city ours, he never stood
       To ease his breast with panting.

MENENIUS   Worthy man!

FIRST SENATOR
121   He cannot but with measure fit the honors
       Which we devise him.

COMINIUS   Our spoils he kicked at,
       And looked upon things precious as they were
       The common muck of the world. He covets less
125   Than misery itself would give; rewards
       His deeds with doing them; and is content
127   To spend the time to end it.

MENENIUS   He's right noble.
       Let him be called for.

FIRST SENATOR   Call Coriolanus.

OFFICER
       He doth appear.
              Enter Coriolanus.

MENENIUS
       The Senate, Coriolanus, are well pleased
       To make thee consul.

CORIOLANUS   I do owe them still
       My life and services.

---

109 *mortal* fatal   **110** *shunless* inevitable   **113** *gan* began to   **114** *ready*
alert; *doubled* strengthened   **115** *fatigate* weary   **117** *reeking* steaming
119 *stood* stopped   **121** *with measure* in proportion   **125** *misery* poverty
127 *spend...it* pass his time in killing time

MENENIUS   It then remains
  That you do speak to the people.
CORIOLANUS   I do beseech you,
  Let me o'erleap that custom; for I cannot
  Put on the gown, stand naked, and entreat them   135
  For my wounds' sake to give their suffrage. Please you
  That I may pass this doing.
SICINIUS   Sir, the people
  Must have their voices; neither will they bate   138
  One jot of ceremony.
MENENIUS   Put them not to't.
  Pray you, go fit you to the custom and
  Take to you, as your predecessors have,
  Your honor with your form.   142
CORIOLANUS   It is a part
  That I shall blush in acting, and might well
  Be taken from the people.
BRUTUS [to Sicinius]   Mark you that?
CORIOLANUS
  To brag unto them, 'Thus I did, and thus!'
  Show them th' unaching scars which I should hide,
  As if I had received them for the hire
  Of their breath only!
MENENIUS   Do not stand upon't.   148
  We recommend to you, tribunes of the people,
  Our purpose to them; and to our noble consul
  Wish we all joy and honor.
SENATORS
  To Coriolanus come all joy and honor!
                    Flourish. Cornets. Then exeunt.
                    Manent Sicinius and Brutus.

BRUTUS
  You see how he intends to use the people.
SICINIUS
  May they perceive's intent! He will require them   154

135 *naked* exposed   138 *voices* votes; *bate* abate   142 *form* formality   148
stand insist   154 *require* ask

155 As if he did contemn what he requested
156 Should be in them to give.
  BRUTUS   Come, we'll inform them
157 Of our proceedings here. On th' market-place
    I know they do attend us.   *[Exeunt.]*

*

II, iii   *Enter seven or eight Citizens.*

  FIRST CITIZEN Once if he do require our voices, we
    ought not to deny him.
  SECOND CITIZEN We may, sir, if we will.
4 THIRD CITIZEN We have power in ourselves to do it, but
5   it is a power that we have no power to do; for if he show
    us his wounds and tell us his deeds, we are to put our
    tongues into those wounds and speak for them. So, if he
    tell us his noble deeds, we must also tell him our noble
    acceptance of them. Ingratitude is monstrous; and for
    the multitude to be ingrateful were to make a monster
    of the multitude; of the which we being members,
    should bring ourselves to be monstrous members.
13 FIRST CITIZEN And to make us no better thought of, a
14 little help will serve; for once we stood up about the corn,
15 he himself stuck not to call us the many-headed multi-
    tude.
16 THIRD CITIZEN We have been called so of many; not
17 that our heads are some brown, some black, some abram,
    some bald, but that our wits are so diversely colored;
    and truly I think if all our wits were to issue out of one
    skull, they would fly east, west, north, south, and their
21 consent of one direct way should be at once to all the
    points o' th' compass.

---

155 *contemn* despise   156 *Should . . . give* that they should be willing to give
157 *market-place* the Forum
II, iii The Roman Forum   4 *power* authority   5 *no power* no right   13–14
a little . . . serve not much is needed   14 *once* when   15 *stuck not* did not
hesitate   16 *of* by   17 *abram* auburn   21 *consent . . . way* areement to go
straight

SECOND CITIZEN Think you so? Which way do you
 judge my wit would fly?

THIRD CITIZEN Nay, your wit will not so soon out as
 another man's will; 'tis strongly wedged up in a blockhead; but if it were at liberty, 'twould, sure, southward.

SECOND CITIZEN Why that way?

THIRD CITIZEN To lose itself in a fog; where being three
 parts melted away with rotten dews, the fourth would 30
 return for conscience sake, to help to get thee a wife.

SECOND CITIZEN You are never without your tricks.
 You may, you may!   33

THIRD CITIZEN Are you all resolved to give your voices?
 But that's no matter, the greater part carries it. I say, if 35
 he would incline to the people, there was never a
 worthier man.

 *Enter Coriolanus in a gown of humility, with
 Menenius.*

Here he comes, and in the gown of humility. Mark his
behavior. We are not to stay all together, but to come by
him where he stands, by ones, by twos, and by threes.
He's to make his requests by particulars; wherein every 41
one of us has a single honor, in giving him our own
voices with our own tongues. Therefore follow me, and
I'll direct you how you shall go by him.

ALL Content, content.   *[Exeunt Citizens.]*

MENENIUS
 O sir, you are not right. Have you not known
 The worthiest men have done't?

CORIOLANUS   What must I say?
 'I pray, sir' – Plague upon't! I cannot bring
 My tongue to such a pace. 'Look, sir, my wounds!
 I got them in my country's service, when
 Some certain of your brethren roared and ran
 From th' noise of our own drums.'

MENENIUS   O me, the gods!

---

30 *rotten* unwholesome   33 *You may* go on   35 *greater part* majority   41 *by
particulars* to individuals

75

You must not speak of that. You must desire them
To think upon you.

CORIOLANUS   Think upon me? Hang 'em!
I would they would forget me, like the virtues
56   Which our divines lose by 'em.

MENENIUS   You'll mar all.
I'll leave you. Pray you, speak to 'em, I pray you,
58   In wholesome manner.   *Exit*.

CORIOLANUS   Bid them wash their faces
And keep their teeth clean.
          Enter three of the Citizens.
59   So, here comes a brace.
You know the cause, sir, of my standing here.

THIRD CITIZEN We do, sir. Tell us what hath brought
you to 't.

CORIOLANUS Mine own desert.

SECOND CITIZEN Your own desert?

CORIOLANUS Ay, not mine own desire.

THIRD CITIZEN How not your own desire?

CORIOLANUS No, sir, 'twas never my desire yet to
trouble the poor with begging.

THIRD CITIZEN You must think, if we give you anything, we hope to gain by you.

CORIOLANUS Well then, I pray, your price o' th' consul-
ship?

FIRST CITIZEN The price is to ask it kindly.

CORIOLANUS Kindly, sir, I pray, let me ha't. I have
74   wounds to show you, which shall be yours in private.
Your good voice, sir. What say you?

SECOND CITIZEN You shall ha't, worthy sir.

77 CORIOLANUS A match, sir. There's in all two worthy
voices begged. I have your alms. Adieu.

THIRD CITIZEN But this is something odd.

SECOND CITIZEN An 'twere to give again – but 'tis no
matter.   *Exeunt*.

56 *lose by* fail to inculcate in   58 *wholesome* decent   59 *brace* pair   74 *yours*
available to you   77 *match* agreement

76

Enter two other Citizens.

CORIOLANUS Pray you now, if it may stand with the tune 81
of your voices that I may be consul, I have here the cus-
tomary gown.

FOURTH CITIZEN You have deserved nobly of your
country, and you have not deserved nobly.

CORIOLANUS Your enigma?

FOURTH CITIZEN You have been a scourge to her
enemies; you have been a rod to her friends. You have
not indeed loved the common people.

CORIOLANUS You should account me the more virtuous
that I have not been common in my love. I will, sir, flatter my sworn brother, the people, to earn a dearer esti- 92
mation of them. 'Tis a condition they account gentle; 93
and since the wisdom of their choice is rather to have my
hat than my heart, I will practice the insinuating nod
and be off to them most counterfeitly: that is, sir, I will 96
counterfeit the bewitchment of some popular man and 97
give it bountiful to the desirers. Therefore, beseech you,
I may be consul.

FIFTH CITIZEN We hope to find you our friend, and
therefore give you our voices heartily.

FOURTH CITIZEN You have received many wounds for
your country.

CORIOLANUS I will not seal your knowledge with show- 103
ing them. I will make much of your voices, and so
trouble you no farther.

BOTH The gods give you joy, sir, heartily!   *[Exeunt.]*

CORIOLANUS
Most sweet voices!
Better it is to die, better to starve,
Than crave the hire which first we do deserve.   109
Why in this wolvish toge should I stand here,   110

---

81 *stand* accord   92–93 *dearer estimation of* higher opinion from   93
condition quality; *gentle* amiable   96 *be off* take my hat off   97 *bewitchment*
witchery; *popular man* man of the people   103 *seal* confirm   109 *hire*
reward; *first* beforehand   110 *toge* toga

77

111 To beg of Hob and Dick that does appear
112 Their needless vouches? Custom calls me to't.
What custom wills, in all things should we do't,
The dust on antique time would lie unswept
And mountainous error be too highly heaped
116 For truth t' o'erpeer. Rather than fool it so,
Let the high office and the honor go
To one that would do thus. I am half through;
The one part suffered, the other will I do.
        Enter three Citizens more.
120 Here come moe voices.
Your voices! For your voices I have fought;
122 Watched for your voices; for your voices bear
Of wounds two dozen odd; battles thrice six
I have seen and heard of; for your voices have
Done many things, some less, some more. Your voices!
Indeed, I would be consul.

FIRST CITIZEN He has done nobly, and cannot go without any honest man's voice.

SECOND CITIZEN Therefore let him be consul. The gods give him joy, and make him good friend to the people!

ALL Amen, amen. God save thee, noble consul! *[Exeunt.]*

CORIOLANUS Worthy voices!
        Enter Menenius, with Brutus and Sicinius.

MENENIUS
133 You have stood your limitation, and the tribunes
134 Endue you with the people's voice. Remains
135 That, in th' official marks invested, you
Anon do meet the Senate.

CORIOLANUS   Is this done?

SICINIUS
The custom of request you have discharged.
The people do admit you, and are summoned

---

111 *Hob* rustic nickname for Robert; *that does appear* as they come by
112 *vouches* attestations   116 *o'erpeer* overtop; *fool it* play the fool   120
moe more   122 *Watched* stayed awake   133 *limitation* appointed time   134
Endue endow; *Remains* it remains   135 *official marks* insignia

To meet anon upon your approbation.   139
CORIOLANUS
Where? at the Senate House?
SICINIUS   There, Coriolanus.
CORIOLANUS
May I change these garments?
SICINIUS   You may, sir.
CORIOLANUS
That I'll straight do; and, knowing myself again,
Repair to th' Senate House.
MENENIUS
I'll keep you company. Will you along?   144
BRUTUS
We stay here for the people.
SICINIUS   Fare you well.
                    Exeunt Coriolanus and Menenius.
He has it now; and by his looks, methinks,
'Tis warm at's heart.
BRUTUS
With a proud heart he wore his humble weeds.
Will you dismiss the people?
                    Enter the Plebeians.
SICINIUS
How now, my masters! Have you chose this man?   150
FIRST CITIZEN
He has our voices, sir.
BRUTUS
We pray the gods he may deserve your loves.
SECOND CITIZEN
Amen, sir. To my poor unworthy notice,
He mocked us when he begged our voices.
THIRD CITIZEN   Certainly
He flouted us downright.
FIRST CITIZEN
No, 'tis his kind of speech; he did not mock us.

139 *upon your approbation* to confirm your election   144 *along* come along
150 *my masters* gentlemen

79

SECOND CITIZEN
Not one amongst us, save yourself, but says
He used us scornfully. He should have showed us
159 His marks of merit, wounds received for's country.
SICINIUS
Why, so he did, I am sure.
ALL   No, no! No man saw 'em.
THIRD CITIZEN
He said he had wounds, which he could show in private;
And with his hat, thus waving it in scorn,
163 'I would be consul,' says he. 'Aged custom,
But by your voices, will not so permit me.
Your voices therefore.' When we granted that,
Here was 'I thank you for your voices, thank you!
Your most sweet voices! Now you have left your voices,
168 I have no further with you.' Was not this mockery?
SICINIUS
169 Why either were you ignorant to see it,
Or, seeing it, of such childish friendliness
To yield your voices?
BRUTUS   Could you not have told him
172 As you were lessoned? When he had no power,
But was a petty servant to the state,
He was your enemy, ever spake against
175 Your liberties and the charters that you bear
176 I' th' body of the weal; and now, arriving
A place of potency and sway o' th' state,
If he should still malignantly remain
179 Fast foe to th' plebeii, your voices might
Be curses to yourselves. You should have said
That as his worthy deeds did claim no less
Than what he stood for, so his gracious nature

159 *for's* for his   163 *Aged* ancient   168 *no further* nothing further to do
169 *ignorant* too unobservant   172 *lessoned* taught   175 *charters* rights
176 *body of the weal* commonwealth; *arriving* attaining   179 *plebeii*
plebeians (Latin)

Would think upon you for your voices and 183
Translate his malice towards you into love, 184
Standing your friendly lord.
SICINIUS   Thus to have said,
As you were fore-advised, had touched his spirit 186
And tried his inclination; from him plucked
Either his gracious promise, which you might,
As cause had called you up, have held him to; 189
Or else it would have galled his surly nature,
Which easily endures not article 191
Tying him to aught; so putting him to rage,
You should have ta'en the advantage of his choler
And passed him unelected.
BRUTUS   Did you perceive
He did solicit you in free contempt 195
When he did need your loves, and do you think
That his contempt shall not be bruising to you
When he hath power to crush? Why, had your bodies
No heart among you? Or had you tongues to cry 199
Against the rectorship of judgment? 200
SICINIUS   Have you,
Ere now, denied the asker? And now again,
Of him that did not ask but mock, bestow 202
Your sued-for tongues! 203
THIRD CITIZEN
He's not confirmed; we may deny him yet.
SECOND CITIZEN
And will deny him.
I'll have five hundred voices of that sound.
FIRST CITIZEN
I twice five hundred, and their friends to piece 'em. 207

183 *Would think upon* should remember 184 *Translate* change 186
fore-advised previously advised; *had* would have 189 *As . . . up* as occasion
aroused you 191–92 *article . . . aught* any conditions 195 *free* open 199
heart courage; *cry* protest 200 *rectorship* rule 202 *bestow* to bestow 203
sued-for solicited 207 *piece* supplement
81

BRUTUS

    Get you hence instantly, and tell those friends
    They have chose a consul that will from them take
    Their liberties ; make them of no more voice
    Than dogs, that are as often beat for barking
212   As therefore kept to do so.

    SICINIUS   Let them assemble,
    And on a safer judgment all revoke
214   Your ignorant election. Enforce his pride,
215   And his old hate unto you. Besides, forget not
    With what contempt he wore the humble weed,
    How in his suit he scorned you ; but your loves,
    Thinking upon his services, took from you
219   Th' apprehension of his present portance,
    Which most gibingly, ungravely, he did fashion
    After th' inveterate hate he bears you.

221 **BRUTUS**   Lay
    A fault on us, your tribunes : that we labored,
223   No impediment between, but that you must
    Cast your election on him.

    SICINIUS   Say you chose him
225   More after our commandment than as guided
    By your own true affections, and that your minds,
    Preoccupied with what you rather must do
    Than what you should, made you against the grain
229   To voice him consul. Lay the fault on us.

    BRUTUS

    Ay, spare us not. Say we read lectures to you,
    How youngly he began to serve his country,
    How long continued, and what stock he springs of,
    The noble house o' th' Marcians, from whence came
234   That Ancus Marcius, Numa's daughter's son,

---

212 *therefore* for that reason   214 *Enforce* emphasize   215 *forget not* do
not ignore   219 *apprehension* observation; *portance* bearing   221-22
Lay . . . on blame   223 *No impediment between* that there should be no
obstacle   225 *after* according to   229 *voice* vote   234 *Numa* second king
of Rome

Who after great Hostilius here was king;
Of the same house Publius and Quintus were,
That our best water brought by conduits hither;   237
And [Censorinus,] nobly namèd so,
Twice being [by the people chosen] censor,   239
Was his great ancestor.
SICINIUS   One thus descended,
That hath beside well in his person wrought
To be set high in place, we did commend
To your remembrances; but you have found,
Scaling his present bearing with his past,   244
That he's your fixèd enemy, and revoke
Your sudden approbation.
BRUTUS   Say, you ne'er had done 't –
Harp on that still – but by our putting on;   247
And presently, when you have drawn your number,   248
Repair to th' Capitol.
ALL   We will so: almost all
Repent in their election.   *Exeunt Plebeians.*
BRUTUS   Let them go on.
This mutiny were better put in hazard   251
Than stay past doubt, for greater.   252
If, as his nature is, he fall in rage
With their refusal, both observe and answer   254
The vantage of his anger.
SICINIUS   To th' Capitol, come.
We will be there before the stream o' th' people;
And this shall seem, as partly 'tis, their own,
Which we have goaded onward.   *Exeunt.*

*

237 *conduits* aqueducts   239 *censor* keeper of public records   244 *Scaling*
weighing   247 *putting on* instigation   248 *presently* immediately; *drawn
your number* gathered a crowd   251 *put in hazard* risked   252 *for greater*
and run a greater risk   254–55 *answer The vantage* take advantage

III, i   *Cornets. Enter Coriolanus, Menenius, all the*
Gentry, Cominius, Titus Lartius, and other
Senators.

CORIOLANUS

1   Tullus Aufidius then had made new head?

LARTIUS

He had, my lord, and that it was which caused
3   Our swifter composition.

CORIOLANUS

So then the Volsces stand but as at first,
5   Ready, when time shall prompt them, to make road
Upon's again.

COMINIUS   They are worn, lord consul, so,
That we shall hardly in our ages see
Their banners wave again.

CORIOLANUS   Saw you Aufidius?

LARTIUS

9   On safeguard he came to me; and did curse
10 Against the Volsces, for they had so vilely
11 Yielded the town. He is retired to Antium.

CORIOLANUS

Spoke he of me?

LARTIUS   He did, my lord.

CORIOLANUS   How? what?

LARTIUS

How often he had met you, sword to sword;
That of all things upon the earth he hated
Your person most; that he would pawn his fortunes
16 To hopeless restitution, so he might
Be called your vanquisher.

CORIOLANUS   At Antium lives he?

III, i A Roman street   1 *made new head* raised another army   3 *swifter composition* coming to terms the more speedily   5 *road* inroads   9 *safeguard* safe-conduct   10 *for* because   11 *Antium* Volscian capital   16 *To hopeless restitution* beyond hope of recovery

LARTIUS
At Antium.

CORIOLANUS
I wish I had a cause to seek him there,
To oppose his hatred fully. Welcome home.
Enter Sicinius and Brutus.
Behold, these are the tribunes of the people,
The tongues o' th' common mouth. I do despise them;
For they do prank them in authority   23
Against all noble sufferance.   24

SICINIUS   Pass no further.

CORIOLANUS
Ha! What is that?

BRUTUS
It will be dangerous to go on. No further.

CORIOLANUS
What makes this change?

MENENIUS
The matter?

COMINIUS
Hath he not passed the noble and the common?   29

BRUTUS
Cominius, no.

CORIOLANUS   Have I had children's voices?

FIRST SENATOR
Tribunes, give way. He shall to th' market-place.

BRUTUS
The people are incensed against him.

SICINIUS   Stop,
Or all will fall in broil.

CORIOLANUS   Are these your herd?
Must these have voices, that can yield them now
And straight disclaim their tongues? What are your
    offices?

23 *prank* dress up   24 *noble sufferance* patrician endurance   29 *passed* been
approved by

36   You being their mouths, why rule you not their teeth?
        Have you not set them on?

MENENIUS   Be calm, be calm.

CORIOLANUS
        It is a purposed thing, and grows by plot,
        To curb the will of the nobility.
40   Suffer't, and live with such as cannot rule
        Nor ever will be ruled.

BRUTUS   Call't not a plot:
        The people cry you mocked them; and of late,
43   When corn was given them gratis, you repined;
44   Scandaled the suppliants for the people, called them
45   Time-pleasers, flatterers, foes to nobleness.

CORIOLANUS
        Why, this was known before.

BRUTUS   Not to them all.

CORIOLANUS
47   Have you informed them sithence?

BRUTUS   How! I inform them!

CORIOLANUS
        You are like to do such business.

BRUTUS   Not unlike,
49   Each way, to better yours.

CORIOLANUS
        Why then should I be consul? By yond clouds,
        Let me deserve so ill as you, and make me
        Your fellow tribune.

SICINIUS   You show too much of that
53   For which the people stir. If you will pass
        To where you are bound, you must inquire your way,
55   Which you are out of, with a gentler spirit,
        Or never be so noble as a consul,
57   Nor yoke with him for tribune.

---

36 *rule* control   40 *live* you will live   43 *repined* expressed regret   44
Scandaled defamed   45 *nobleness* aristocracy   47 *sithence* since   49 *better
yours* do better than you would do as consul   53 *For . . . stir* which disturbs
the people   55 *are out of* have strayed from   57 *yoke* cooperate

MENENIUS   Let's be calm.

COMINIUS

The people are abused, set on. This paltering   58
Becomes not Rome, nor has Coriolanus
Deserved this so dishonored rub, laid falsely   60
I' th' plain way of his merit.

CORIOLANUS   Tell me of corn!
This was my speech, and I will speak't again —

MENENIUS
Not now, not now.

FIRST SENATOR   Not in this heat, sir, now.

CORIOLANUS
Now, as I live, I will. My nobler friends,
I crave their pardons.
For the mutable, rank-scented meiny, let them   66
Regard me as I do not flatter, and
Therein behold themselves. I say again,
In soothing them we nourish 'gainst our Senate
The cockle of rebellion, insolence, sedition,   70
Which we ourselves have ploughed for, sowed, and
    scattered
By mingling them with us, the honored number,
Who lack not virtue, no, nor power, but that
Which they have given to beggars.

MENENIUS   Well, no more.

FIRST SENATOR
No more words, we beseech you.

CORIOLANUS   How? no more?
As for my country I have shed my blood,
Not fearing outward force, so shall my lungs
Coin words till their decay against those measles   78
Which we disdain should tetter us, yet sought   79
The very way to catch them.

BRUTUS   You speak o' th' people

---

58 *abused* deceived; *paltering* equivocating   **60** *dishonored rub* shameful
obstacle   **66** *For* as for; *meiny* multitude   **70** *cockle* weed   **78** *those
measles* that leprosy   **79** *tetter* break out in; *sought* have sought

      As if you were a god to punish, not
      A man of their infirmity.

SICINIUS   'Twere well
      We let the people know't.

MENENIUS   What, what? His choler?

CORIOLANUS
      Choler!
      Were I as patient as the midnight sleep,
      By Jove, 'twould be my mind!

SICINIUS   It is a mind
      That shall remain a poison where it is,
      Not poison any further.

CORIOLANUS   Shall remain!
89   Hear you this Triton of the minnows? Mark you
      His absolute 'shall'?

90 COMINIUS   'Twas from the canon.

CORIOLANUS   'Shall'?
      O good but most unwise patricians! Why,
      You grave but reckless senators, have you thus
93   Given Hydra here to choose an officer,
      That with his peremptory 'shall,' being but
95   The horn and noise o' th' monster's, wants not spirit
      To say he'll turn your current in a ditch,
      And make your channel his? If he have power,
98   Then vail your ignorance; if none, awake
99   Your dangerous lenity. If you are learned,
      Be not as common fools; if you are not,
101   Let them have cushions by you. You are plebeians
      If they be senators; and they are no less
103   When, both your voices blended, the great'st taste
104   Most palates theirs. They choose their magistrate;
      And such a one as he, who puts his 'shall,'

---

89 *Triton* god who calms the waves   90 *from the canon* contrary to rule   93
Given allowed; *Hydra* many-headed monster   95 *horn* (attribute of Triton)
98 *vail your ignorance* let your negligence bow down   99 *lenity* mildness
101 *have cushions by you* sit with you in the Senate   103 *great'st taste* taste
of the greatest   104 *palates* smacks of

His popular 'shall,' against a graver bench
Than ever frowned in Greece. By Jove himself,
It makes the consuls base ! and my soul aches
To know, when two authorities are up,   109
Neither supreme, how soon confusion
May enter 'twixt the gap of both and take
The one by th' other.
COMINIUS   Well, on to th' market-place.
CORIOLANUS
Whoever gave that counsel, to give forth
The corn o' th' storehouse gratis, as 'twas used
Sometime in Greece –
MENENIUS   Well, well, no more of that.
CORIOLANUS
Though there the people had more absolute power –
I say they nourished disobedience, fed
The ruin of the state.
BRUTUS   Why, shall the people give
One that speaks thus their voice ?
CORIOLANUS   I'll give my reasons,
More worthier than their voices. They know the corn
Was not our recompense, resting well assured   121
They ne'er did service for't. Being pressed to th' war,   122
Even when the navel of the state was touched,   123
They would not thread the gates. This kind of service   124
Did not deserve corn gratis. Being i' th' war,
Their mutinies and revolts, wherein they showed
Most valor, spoke not for them. Th' accusation
Which they have often made against the Senate,
All cause unborn, could never be the native   129
Of our so frank donation. Well, what then ?   130
How shall this bosom multiplied digest   131
The Senate's courtesy ? Let deeds express

---

109 *up* in action   121 *recompense* reward to them   122 *pressed* conscripted
123 *navel* center   124 *thread* pass through   129 *All cause unborn* without
justification; *native* origin   130 *frank* free   131 *bosom multiplied* many-
breasted crowd

What's like to be their words : 'We did request it ;

134 We are the greater poll, and in true fear
They gave us our demands.' Thus we debase
The nature of our seats, and make the rabble
Call our cares fears ; which will in time
Break ope the locks o' th' Senate, and bring in
The crows to peck the eagles.

MENENIUS   Come, enough.

BRUTUS
Enough, with over-measure.

CORIOLANUS   No, take more !
What may be sworn by, both divine and human,

142 Seal what I end withal ! This double worship,
Where one part does disdain with cause, the other

144 Insult without all reason ; where gentry, title, wisdom,
Cannot conclude but by the yea and no

146 Of general ignorance – it must omit
Real necessities, and give way the while

148 To unstable slightness. Purpose so barred, it follows,
Nothing is done to purpose. Therefore, beseech you, –

150 You that will be less fearful than discreet ;
That love the fundamental part of state

152 More than you doubt the change on't ; that prefer
A noble life before a long, and wish

154 To jump a body with a dangerous physic
That's sure of death without it – at once pluck out
The multitudinous tongue ; let them not lick

157 The sweet which is their poison. Your dishonor
Mangles true judgment, and bereaves the state

159 Of that integrity which should become't,
Not having the power to do the good it would
For th' ill which doth control't.

---

134 *greater poll* majority   142 *Seal* confirm; *withal* with; *double worship*
divided authority   144 *without* beyond   146 *omit* neglect   148 *Purpose so
barred* when planning thus becomes impossible   150 *discreet* wise   152
doubt fear   154 *jump* risk   157 *sweet* flattery   159 *integrity* wholeness;
become't befit it

BRUTUS   'Has said enough.   161
SICINIUS
    'Has spoken like a traitor, and shall answer
    As traitors do.
CORIOLANUS   Thou wretch, despite o'erwhelm thee!   163
    What should the people do with these bald tribunes?
    On whom depending, their obedience fails
    To th' greater bench. In a rebellion,   166
    When what's not meet, but what must be, was law,
    Then were they chosen. In a better hour,
    Let what is meet be said it must be meet,   169
    And throw their power i' th' dust.
BRUTUS
    Manifest treason!
SICINIUS   This a consul? No.
BRUTUS
    The aediles, ho!   172
        Enter an Aedile.
            Let him be apprehended.
SICINIUS
    Go, call the people; *[exit Aedile]* in whose name myself
    Attach thee as a traitorous innovator,   174
    A foe to th' public weal. Obey, I charge thee,
    And follow to thine answer.   176
CORIOLANUS   Hence, old goat!
ALL [PATRICIANS]
    We'll surety him.   177
COMINIUS   Ag'd sir, hands off.
CORIOLANUS
    Hence, rotten thing! or I shall shake thy bones
    Out of thy garments.
SICINIUS   Help, ye citizens!

---

161 *'Has* he has   163 *despite* scorn   166 *greater bench* Senate   169 *Let . . .
be meet* let it be said that what is proper should be done   172 *aediles* police
officers   174 *Attach* arrest   176 *answer* interrogation   177 *surety* stand
pledged for

Enter a rabble of Plebeians, with the Aediles.

MENENIUS
On both sides more respect.

SICINIUS
Here's he that would take from you all your power.

BRUTUS
Seize him, aediles!

ALL [PLEBEIANS]
Down with him! down with him!

SECOND SENATOR
Weapons, weapons, weapons!
   They all bustle about Coriolanus.

ALL
Tribunes! – Patricians! – Citizens! – What, ho!
Sicinius! – Brutus! – Coriolanus! – Citizens!
Peace, peace, peace! – Stay, hold, peace!

MENENIUS
What is about to be? I am out of breath;
189   Confusion's near; I cannot speak. You, tribunes
To th' people! – Coriolanus, patience! –
Speak, good Sicinius.

SICINIUS   Hear me, people. Peace!

ALL [PLEBEIANS] Let's hear our tribune. Peace! Speak,
speak, speak!

SICINIUS
194   You are at point to lose your liberties.
Marcius would have all from you, Marcius,
Whom late you have named for consul.

MENENIUS   Fie, fie, fie!
This is the way to kindle, not to quench.

FIRST SENATOR
To unbuild the city and to lay all flat.

SICINIUS
What is the city but the people?

---

189 *Confusion* ruin   194 *at point to lose* on the point of losing

ALL [PLEBEIANS]   True,
   The people are the city.
BRUTUS
   By the consent of all we were established
   The people's magistrates.
ALL [PLEBEIANS]   You so remain.
MENENIUS
   And so are like to do.
COMINIUS
   That is the way to lay the city flat,
   To bring the roof to the foundation,
   And bury all, which yet distinctly ranges,   206
   In heaps and piles of ruin.
SICINIUS   This deserves death.
BRUTUS
   Or let us stand to our authority,
   Or let us lose it. We do here pronounce,
   Upon the part o' th' people, in whose power
   We were elected theirs, Marcius is worthy
   Of present death.   212
SICINIUS   Therefore lay hold of him;
   Bear him to th' Rock Tarpeian, and from thence   213
   Into destruction cast him.
BRUTUS   Aediles, seize him!
ALL [PLEBEIANS]
   Yield, Marcius, yield!
MENENIUS   Hear me one word.
   Beseech you, tribunes, hear me but a word.
AEDILES
   Peace, peace!
MENENIUS [to Brutus]
   Be that you seem, truly your country's friend,
   And temp'rately proceed to what you would
   Thus violently redress.

206 *distinctly ranges* is ranked separately 212 *present* immediate 213
Rock Tarpeian Capitoline cliff from which state criminals were hurled

BRUTUS   Sir, those cold ways,
That seem like prudent helps, are very poisonous
Where the disease is violent. Lay hands upon him,
And bear him to the Rock.
          Coriolanus draws his sword.
CORIOLANUS   No, I'll die here.
There's some among you have beheld me fighting :
Come, try upon yourselves what you have seen me.
MENENIUS
Down with that sword! Tribunes, withdraw awhile.
BRUTUS
Lay hands upon him.
MENENIUS   Help Marcius, help!
You that be noble, help him, young and old!
ALL [PLEBEIANS]
Down with him! down with him!   *Exeunt.*
          *In this mutiny the Tribunes, the Aediles, and the
          People are beat in.*
MENENIUS
Go, get you to your house! be gone, away!
231   All will be naught else.
SECOND SENATOR   Get you gone.
CORIOLANUS   Stand fast!
We have as many friends as enemies.
MENENIUS
Shall it be put to that?
FIRST SENATOR   The gods forbid!
I prithee, noble friend, home to thy house ;
Leave us to cure this cause.
MENENIUS   For 'tis a sore upon us
236   You cannot tent yourself. Be gone, beseech you.
COMINIUS
Come, sir, along with us.
CORIOLANUS
I would they were barbarians, as they are,

231 *naught* ruined   236 *tent* treat

ALL [PLEBEIANS]
  No, no, no, no, no!
MENENIUS
  If, by the tribunes' leave, and yours, good people,
  I may be heard, I would crave a word or two;
  The which shall turn you to no further harm   283
  Than so much loss of time.
SICINIUS   Speak briefly then;
  For we are peremptory to dispatch   285
  This viperous traitor. To eject him hence
  Were but our danger, and to keep him here
  Our certain death. Therefore it is decreed
  He dies to-night.
MENENIUS   Now the good gods forbid
  That our renownèd Rome, whose gratitude
  Towards her deservèd children is enrolled   291
  In Jove's own book, like an unnatural dam
  Should now eat up her own!
SICINIUS
  He's a disease that must be cut away.
MENENIUS
  O, he's a limb that has but a disease:
  Mortal, to cut it off; to cure it, easy.
  What has he done to Rome that's worthy death?   297
  Killing our enemies, the blood he hath lost –
  Which, I dare vouch, is more than that he hath,
  By many an ounce – he dropped it for his country;
  And what is left, to lose it by his country
  Were to us all that do't and suffer it
  A brand to th' end o' th' world.
SICINIUS   This is clean kam.   303
BRUTUS
  Merely awry. When he did love his country,   304
  It honored him.

283 *turn you to* cause you   285 *peremptory* resolved   291 *deservèd* meritori-
ous   291–92 *enrolled . . . book* recorded in the Capitol   297 *worthy* deserving of   303 *clean kam* quite wrong   304 *Merely awry* completely twisted

SICINIUS   The service of the foot,
Being once gangrened, is not then respected
For what before it was.
BRUTUS   We'll hear no more.
Pursue him to his house and pluck him thence,
Lest his infection, being of catching nature,
Spread further.
MENENIUS   One word more, one word.
This tiger-footed rage, when it shall find
312   The harm of unscanned swiftness, will too late
313   Tie leaden pounds to's heels. Proceed by process,
Lest parties, as he is beloved, break out
And sack great Rome with Romans.
BRUTUS   If it were so –
SICINIUS
What do ye talk?
Have we not had a taste of his obedience?
318   Our aediles smote? ourselves resisted? Come.
MENENIUS
Consider this: he has been bred i' th' wars
Since 'a could draw a sword, and is ill schooled
321   In bolted language; meal and bran together
He throws without distinction. Give me leave,
I'll go to him and undertake to bring him
324   Where he shall answer by a lawful form,
In peace, to his utmost peril.
FIRST SENATOR   Noble tribunes,
It is the humane way. The other course
Will prove too bloody, and the end of it
Unknown to the beginning.
SICINIUS   Noble Menenius,
Be you then as the people's officer.
Masters, lay down your weapons.
BRUTUS   Go not home.

---

312 *unscanned swiftness* thoughtless haste   313 *to's* to its; *process* course of
law   318 *smote* smitten   321 *bolted* sifted   324–25 *answer . . . peril* peace-
fully face judgment, however severe

SICINIUS
    Meet on the market-place. We'll attend you there ;   331
    Where, if you bring not Marcius, we'll proceed
    In our first way.
MENENIUS   I'll bring him to you.
    [To the Senators]
    Let me desire your company. He must come,
    Or what is worst will follow.
FIRST SENATOR   Pray you, let's to him.   335
                 Exeunt omnes.

*

    Enter Coriolanus, with Nobles.   III, ii
CORIOLANUS
    Let them pull all about mine ears, present me
    Death on the wheel or at wild horses' heels,   2
    Or pile ten hills on the Tarpeian Rock,
    That the precipitation might down stretch   4
    Below the beam of sight, yet will I still   5
    Be thus to them.
NOBLE   You do the nobler.
CORIOLANUS
    I muse my mother   7
    Does not approve me further, who was wont
    To call them woollen vassals, things created
    To buy and sell with groats, to show bare heads   10
    In congregations, to yawn, be still and wonder,   11
    When one but of my ordinance stood up   12
    To speak of peace or war.
    Enter Volumnia.   I talk of you :
    Why did you wish me milder ? Would you have me

331 *attend* await 335 *to* go to
III, ii The house of Coriolanus 2 *wheel* instrument of torture 4 *pre-cipitation* precipitousness 5 *Below . . . sight* beyond eyesight 7 *muse* wonder that 10 *groats* fourpenny pieces 11 *congregations* assemblies 12 *ordinance* rank

False to my nature? Rather say I play
The man I am.

VOLUMNIA   O, sir, sir, sir,
I would have had you put your power well on,
Before you had worn it out.

18 CORIOLANUS   Let go.

VOLUMNIA
You might have been enough the man you are
With striving less to be so. Lesser had been
21 The taxings of your dispositions, if
You had not showed them how ye were disposed
23 Ere they lacked power to cross you.

CORIOLANUS   Let them hang!

VOLUMNIA
Ay, and burn too!
    Enter Menenius, with the Senators.

MENENIUS
25 Come, come, you have been too rough, something too
        rough.
You must return and mend it.

FIRST SENATOR   There's no remedy,
Unless, by not so doing, our good city
28 Cleave in the midst, and perish.

VOLUMNIA   Pray, be counselled.
29 I have a heart as little apt as yours,
But yet a brain that leads my use of anger
31 To better vantage.

MENENIUS   Well said, noble woman!
Before he should thus stoop to th' herd, but that
33 The violent fit o' th' time craves it as physic
For the whole state, I would put mine armor on,
Which I can scarcely bear.

CORIOLANUS   What must I do?

---

18 *Let go* desist   21 *dispositions* inclinations   23 *Ere they lacked* before they
lost   25 *something* somewhat   28 *Cleave . . . midst* divide in the middle
29 *apt* compliant   31 *vantage* advantage   33 *physic* medicine

MENENIUS
  Return to th' tribunes.
CORIOLANUS   Well, what then? what then?
MENENIUS
  Repent what you have spoke.
CORIOLANUS
  For them? I cannot do it to the gods.
  Must I then do't to them?
VOLUMNIA   You are too absolute;
  Though therein you can never be too noble,
  But when extremities speak. I have heard you say,   41
  Honor and policy, like unsevered friends,   42
  I' th' war do grow together. Grant that, and tell me,
  In peace what each of them by th' other lose,
  That they combine not there.
CORIOLANUS   Tush, tush!
MENENIUS   A good demand.
VOLUMNIA
  If it be honor in your wars to seem
  The same you are not, – which, for your best ends,
  You adopt your policy – how is it less or worse,   48
  That it shall hold companionship in peace
  With honor, as in war; since that to both   50
  It stands in like request?
CORIOLANUS   Why force you this?   51
VOLUMNIA
  Because that now it lies you on to speak   52
  To th' people, not by your own instruction,
  Nor by th' matter which your heart prompts you,
  But with such words that are but roted in   55
  Your tongue, though but bastards and syllables
  Of no allowance to your bosom's truth.   57

---

41 *extremities speak* necessity prompts **42** *policy* strategy; *unsevered* inseparable **48** *adopt* adopt as **50–51** *since . . . request* since it is equally necessary to both **51** *force* urge **52** *lies you on* is incumbent upon you **55** *roted* memorized **57** *Of . . . truth* unsanctioned by your real feelings

Now, this no more dishonors you at all
59   Than to take in a town with gentle words,
Which else would put you to your fortune and
The hazard of much blood.
I would dissemble with my nature where
My fortunes and my friends at stake required
64   I should do so in honor. I am in this
Your wife, your son, these senators, the nobles ;
66   And you will rather show our general louts
67   How you can frown than spend a fawn upon 'em,
68   For the inheritance of their loves and safeguard
69   Of what that want might ruin.
MENENIUS   Noble lady ! –
Come, go with us. Speak fair. You may salve so,
71   Not what is dangerous present, but the loss
Of what is past.
VOLUMNIA   I prithee now, my son,
Go to them, with this bonnet in thy hand ;
74   And thus far having stretched it, – here be with them –
75   Thy knee bussing the stones, – for in such business
Action is eloquence, and the eyes of th' ignorant
77   More learned than the ears – waving thy head,
78   Which, often thus correcting thy stout heart,
79   Now humble as the ripest mulberry
That will not hold the handling ; or say to them
Thou art their soldier, and being bred in broils
Hast not the soft way which, thou dost confess,
Were fit for thee to use as they to claim,
In asking their good loves ; but thou wilt frame
85   Thyself, forsooth, hereafter theirs, so far
As thou hast power and person.
MENENIUS   This but done,

---

59 *take in* capture   64 *am* speak for   66 *general* common   67 *fawn* flat-
tering appeal   68 *inheritance* obtainment   69 *that want* the lack of their
loves   71–72 *Not . . . past* not only immediate danger but past loss   74 *here
. . . them* treat them thus   75 *bussing* kissing (vulgar)   77 *waving* bowing
78 *correcting* chastening   79 *humble* abase   85 *theirs* to suit them

Even as she speaks, why, their hearts were yours;   87
For they have pardons, being asked, as free
As words to little purpose.   89
VOLUMNIA   Prithee now,
  Go, and be ruled; although I know thou hadst rather   90
  Follow thine enemy in a fiery gulf   91
  Than flatter him in a bower.   92
      Enter Cominius.   Here is Cominius.
COMINIUS
  I have been i' th' market-place; and, sir, 'tis fit
  You make strong party, or defend yourself
  By calmness or by absence. All's in anger.
MENENIUS
  Only fair speech.
COMINIUS   I think 'twill serve, if he
  Can thereto frame his spirit.
VOLUMNIA   He must, and will.
  Prithee now, say you will, and go about it.
CORIOLANUS
  Must I go show them my unbarbed sconce? Must I   99
  With my base tongue give to my noble heart
  A lie that it must bear? Well, I will do't.
  Yet, were there but this single plot to lose,   102
  This mould of Marcius, they to dust should grind it   103
  And throw't against the wind. To th' market-place!
  You have put me now to such a part which never
  I shall discharge to th' life.   106
COMINIUS   Come, come, we'll prompt you.
VOLUMNIA
  I prithee now, sweet son, as thou hast said
  My praises made thee first a soldier, so,
  To have my praise for this, perform a part
  Thou hast not done before.

---

87 *were* would be   89 *words . . . purpose* a trifling concession   90 *ruled*
advised   91 *in* into   92 *bower* boudoir   99 *unbarbed sconce* uncovered head
102 *plot* piece of earth   103 *mould* form   106 *discharge . . . life* enact con-
vincingly

CORIOLANUS   Well, I must do't.
Away, my disposition, and possess me
Some harlot's spirit! My throat of war be turned,
113   Which quired with my drum, into a pipe
Small as an eunuch, or the virgin voice
115   That babies lulls asleep! The smiles of knaves
116   Tent in my cheeks, and schoolboys' tears take up
117   The glasses of my sight! A beggar's tongue
Make motion through my lips, and my armed knees,
Who bowed but in my stirrup, bend like his
That hath received an alms! I will not do't,
121   Lest I surcease to honor mine own truth
And by my body's action teach my mind
123   A most inherent baseness.

VOLUMNIA   At thy choice, then.
To beg of thee, it is my more dishonor
Than thou of them. Come all to ruin! Let
Thy mother rather feel thy pride than fear
127   Thy dangerous stoutness; for I mock at death
128   With as big heart as thou. Do as thou list.
Thy valiantness was mine, thou suck'st it from me;
130   But owe thy pride thyself.

CORIOLANUS   Pray, be content.
Mother, I am going to the market-place.
132   Chide me no more. I'll mountebank their loves,
133   Cog their hearts from them, and come home beloved
Of all the trades in Rome. Look, I am going.
Commend me to my wife. I'll return consul,
Or never trust to what my tongue can do
I' th' way of flattery further.

VOLUMNIA   Do your will.

                                        Exit Volumnia.

---

113 *quired* sang in chorus   115 *babies lulls* lulls dolls   116 *Tent* encamp;
take up occupy   117 *glasses . . . sight* eyeballs   121 *surcease* cease   123
inherent irremovable   127 *dangerous stoutness* danger provoked by your
obstinacy   128 *thou list* you please   130 *owe* you own   132 *mountebank*
gain by artful speeches   133 *Cog* cheat

COMINIUS
    Away! The tribunes do attend you. Arm yourself
    To answer mildly; for they are prepared
    With accusations, as I hear, more strong
    Than are upon you yet.

CORIOLANUS
    The word is 'mildly.' Pray you, let us go.   142
    Let them accuse me by invention, I   143
    Will answer in mine honor.   144

MENENIUS   Ay, but mildly.

CORIOLANUS
    Well, mildly be't then. Mildly!   *Exeunt.*

*

    Enter Sicinius and Brutus.   III, iii

BRUTUS
    In this point charge him home, that he affects   1
    Tyrannical power. If he evade us there,
    Enforce him with his envy to the people,   3
    And that the spoil got on the Antiates
    Was ne'er distributed.
        Enter an Aedile. What, will he come?

AEDILE
    He's coming.

BRUTUS   How accompanied?

AEDILE
    With old Menenius, and those senators
    That always favored him.

SICINIUS   Have you a catalogue
    Of all the voices that we have procured
    Set down by th' poll?   10

AEDILE   I have; 'tis ready.

---

142 *word* watchword   143 *accuse . . . invention* invent accusations against me
144 *in* according to
III, iii The Roman Forum   1 *charge him home* press the charge against
him; *affects* aims at   3 *Enforce* confront; *envy to* ill-will toward   10 *poll*
registry of voters

SICINIUS
Have you collected them by tribes?

AEDILE   I have.

SICINIUS
Assemble presently the people hither;
And when they hear me say, 'It shall be so
I' th' right and strength o' th' commons,' be it either
For death, for fine, or banishment, then let them,
If I say fine, cry 'Fine!' – if death, cry 'Death!',
Insisting on the old prerogative
18   And power i' th' truth o' th' cause.

AEDILE   I shall inform them.

BRUTUS
19   And when such time they have begun to cry,
Let them not cease, but with a din confused
Enforce the present execution
Of what we chance to sentence.

AEDILE   Very well.

SICINIUS
23   Make them be strong, and ready for this hint
24   When we shall hap to give't them.

BRUTUS   Go about it.
                                    [Exit Aedile.]
Put him to choler straight. He hath been used
26   Ever to conquer, and to have his worth
Of contradiction. Being once chafed, he cannot
Be reined again to temperance; then he speaks
29   What's in his heart, and that is there which looks
With us to break his neck.
            Enter Coriolanus, Menenius, and Cominius, with
            others.

SICINIUS   Well, here he comes.

MENENIUS
Calmly, I do beseech you.

18 *truth . . . cause* justice of the case   19 *when such time* in such time as; *cry*
shout   23 *hint* occasion   24 *hap* chance   26 *worth* pennyworth   29 *looks*
tends

CORIOLANUS
Ay, as an ostler, that for th' poorest piece   32
Will bear the knave by th' volume. Th' honored gods   33
Keep Rome in safety, and the chairs of justice
Supplied with worthy men! plant love among's!
Throng our large temples with the shows of peace,   36
And not our streets with war!
FIRST SENATOR   Amen, amen.
MENENIUS
A noble wish.
        Enter the Aedile, with the Plebeians.
SICINIUS
Draw near, ye people.
AEDILE
List to your tribunes. Audience! Peace, I say!   40
CORIOLANUS
First hear me speak.
BOTH TRIBUNES   Well, say. Peace, ho!
CORIOLANUS
Shall I be charged no further than this present?   42
Must all determine here?   43
SICINIUS   I do demand,
If you submit you to the people's voices,
Allow their officers, and are content   45
To suffer lawful censure for such faults
As shall be proved upon you?
CORIOLANUS   I am content.
MENENIUS
Lo, citizens, he says he is content.
The warlike service he has done, consider; think
Upon the wounds his body bears, which show   50
Like graves i' th' holy churchyard.
CORIOLANUS   Scratches with briars,

32 *piece* coin   33 *bear . . . volume* allow himself to be called knave repeatedly
36 *shows* ceremonies   40 *List* listen; *Audience* hearing   42 *this present* the
moment   43 *determine* end   45 *Allow* acknowledge   50 *Upon* about

Scars to move laughter only.

MENENIUS   Consider further,
That when he speaks not like a citizen,
You find him like a soldier. Do not take
His rougher accents for malicious sounds,
But, as I say, such as become a soldier,
57   Rather than envy you.

COMINIUS   Well, well, no more.

CORIOLANUS
What is the matter
That being passed for consul with full voice,
I am so dishonored that the very hour
You take it off again?

61 SICINIUS   Answer to us.

CORIOLANUS
62   Say, then. 'Tis true, I ought so.

SICINIUS
We charge you that you have contrived to take
64   From Rome all seasoned office, and to wind
Yourself into a power tyrannical,
For which you are a traitor to the people.

CORIOLANUS
How? traitor?

MENENIUS   Nay, temperately! your promise.

CORIOLANUS
68   The fires i' th' lowest hell fold in the people!
69   Call me their traitor, thou injurious tribune!
70   Within thine eyes sat twenty thousand deaths,
In thy hands clutched as many millions, in
Thy lying tongue both numbers, I would say
'Thou liest' unto thee with a voice as free
As I do pray the gods.

SICINIUS   Mark you this, people?

---

57 *envy* show malice toward   61 *Answer to us* i.e. we will ask the questions
62 *so* to do so   64 *seasoned* established   68 *fold in* enfold   69 *injurious*
insulting   70 *Within* if within

108

ALL
  To th' Rock, to th' Rock with him!
SICINIUS   Peace!
  We need not put new matter to his charge.
  What you have seen him do and heard him speak,
  Beating your officers, cursing yourselves,
  Opposing laws with strokes, and here defying
  Those whose great power must try him – even this,
  So criminal and in such capital kind,   81
  Deserves th' extremest death.
BRUTUS   But since he hath
  Served well for Rome –
CORIOLANUS   What do you prate of service?
BRUTUS
  I talk of that, that know it.
CORIOLANUS
  You?
MENENIUS
  Is this the promise that you made your mother?
COMINIUS
  Know, I pray you –
CORIOLANUS   I'll know no further.
  Let them pronounce the steep Tarpeian death,
  Vagabond exile, flaying, pent to linger   89
  But with a grain a day – I would not buy
  Their mercy at the price of one fair word;
  Nor check my courage for what they can give,   92
  To have't with saying 'Good morrow.'
SICINIUS   For that he has,   93
  As much as in him lies, from time to time   94
  Envied against the people, seeking means   95
  To pluck away their power; as now at last   96
  Given hostile strokes, and that not in the presence

81 *capital* punishable by death   89 *pent* were I confined   92 *check* restrain
93 *For that* because   94 *in him lies* he could   95 *Envied against* shown ill-
will toward   96 *as* and because he has

>   Of dreaded justice, but on the ministers
>   That doth distribute it : i' th' name o' th' people
>   And in the power of us the tribunes, we,
>   Even from this instant, banish him our city,
> 102   In peril of precipitation
>   From off the Rock Tarpeian, never more
>   To enter our Rome gates. I' th' people's name,
>   I say it shall be so.

>   ALL
>   It shall be so! it shall be so! Let him away!
>   He's banished, and it shall be so!

>   COMINIUS
>   Hear me, my masters, and my common friends –

>   SICINIUS
>   He's sentenced. No more hearing.

>   COMINIUS   Let me speak.
>   I have been consul, and can show for Rome
>   Her enemies' marks upon me. I do love
>   My country's good with a respect more tender,
>   More holy and profound, than mine own life,
> 114   My dear wife's estimate, her womb's increase,
>   And treasure of my loins. Then if I would
>   Speak that –

>   SICINIUS   We know your drift. Speak what?
>   BRUTUS
> 117   There's no more to be said, but he is banished
>   As enemy to the people and his country.
>   It shall be so.

>   ALL
>   It shall be so! it shall be so!

>   CORIOLANUS
> 121   You common cry of curs, whose breath I hate
> 122   As reek o' th' rotten fens, whose loves I prize
>   As the dead carcasses of unburied men

---

102 *precipitation* being thrown   114 *estimate* value   117 *but* except that
121 *cry* pack   122 *reek* vapor

That do corrupt my air, I banish you !
And here remain with your uncertainty.
Let every feeble rumor shake your hearts !
Your enemies, with nodding of their plumes,
Fan you into despair ! Have the power still
To banish your defenders, till at length
Your ignorance – which finds not till it feels,   130
Making but reservation of yourselves,   131
Still your own foes – deliver you as most
Abated captives to some nation   133
That won you without blows ! Despising,
For you, the city, thus I turn my back.   135
There is a world elsewhere.

>   *Exeunt Coriolanus, Cominius, with Menenius*
>   *[and the other Senators].*

AEDILE
  The people's enemy is gone, is gone !
ALL
  Our enemy is banished ! he is gone !
>   *They all shout, and throw up their caps.*
                              Hoo ! hoo !
SICINIUS
  Go, see him out at gates, and follow him
  As he hath followed you, with all despite ;
  Give him deserved vexation. Let a guard   141
  Attend us through the city.
ALL
  Come, come, let's see him out at gates ! Come.
  The gods preserve our noble tribunes ! Come.   *Exeunt.*

*

130 *finds . . . feels* learns only through experience   131 *Making . . . of*
seeking to preserve only   133 *Abated* humbled   135 *For* because of
141 *vexation* mortification

IV, i   *Enter Coriolanus, Volumnia, Virgilia, Menenius,*
         Cominius, with the young Nobility of Rome.

CORIOLANUS
Come, leave your tears. A brief farewell. The beast
With many heads butts me away. Nay, mother,
3 Where is your ancient courage? You were used
To say extremities was the trier of spirits;
That common chances common men could bear;
That when the sea was calm all boats alike
Showed mastership in floating; fortune's blows
8 When most struck home, being gentle wounded craves
A noble cunning. You were used to load me
With precepts that would make invincible
11 The heart that conned them.

VIRGILIA
O heavens! O heavens!

CORIOLANUS   Nay, I prithee, woman –

VOLUMNIA
Now the red pestilence strike all trades in Rome,
And occupations perish!

CORIOLANUS   What, what, what!
15 I shall be loved when I am lacked. Nay, mother,
Resume that spirit when you were wont to say,
If you had been the wife of Hercules,
Six of his labors you'd have done, and saved
Your husband so much sweat. Cominius,
Droop not; adieu. Farewell, my wife, my mother.
I'll do well yet. Thou old and true Menenius,
22 Thy tears are salter than a younger man's,
23 And venomous to thine eyes. My sometime general,
  I have seen thee stern, and thou hast oft beheld
Heart-hard'ning spectacles. Tell these sad women
26 'Tis fond to wail inevitable strokes,

IV, i Before a gate of Rome 3 *ancient* earlier 8 *being . . . craves* to bear
one's wounds like a gentleman requires 11 *conned* studied 15 *lacked*
missed 22 *salter* saltier 23 *sometime* former 26 *fond* foolish

As 'tis to laugh at 'em. My mother, you wot well   27
My hazards still have been your solace ; and   28
Believe't not lightly – though I go alone,
Like to a lonely dragon, that his fen   30
Makes feared and talked of more than seen – your son
Will or exceed the common or be caught   32
With cautelous baits and practice.   33

VOLUMNIA   My first son,
Whither wilt thou go ? Take good Cominius
With thee awhile. Determine on some course,
More than a wild exposture to each chance   36
That starts i' th' way before thee.

CORIOLANUS   O the gods !

COMINIUS
I'll follow thee a month, devise with thee
Where thou shalt rest, that thou mayst hear of us
And we of thee. So, if the time thrust forth
A cause for thy repeal, we shall not send   41
O'er the vast world to seek a single man,
And lose advantage, which doth ever cool
I' th' absence of the needer.

CORIOLANUS   Fare ye well.
Thou hast years upon thee, and thou art too full
Of the wars' surfeits to go rove with one   46
That's yet unbruised. Bring me but out at gate.   47
Come, my sweet wife, my dearest mother, and
My friends of noble touch. When I am forth,   49
Bid me farewell, and smile. I pray you, come.
While I remain above the ground, you shall
Hear from me still, and never of me aught
But what is like me formerly.

MENENIUS   That's worthily

---

27 *wot* know   28 *still* always   30 *fen* marsh   32 *or . . . common* either be
exceptional   33 *cautelous* crafty; *practice* stratagem   36 *exposture* exposure
41 *repeal* recall   46 *surfeits* excesses   47 *Bring . . . gate* just accompany me
to the gate   49 *noble touch* tested nobility

As any ear can hear. Come, let's not weep.
If I could shake off but one seven-years
From these old arms and legs, by the good gods,
I'd with thee every foot.
CORIOLANUS   Give me thy hand.
Come.   *Exeunt.*

                                *

IV, ii   *Enter the two Tribunes, Sicinius and Brutus, with
              the Aedile.*
SICINIUS
1   Bid them all home. He's gone, and we'll no further.
    The nobility are vexed, whom we see have sided
    In his behalf.
BRUTUS   Now we have shown our power,
    Let us seem humbler after it is done
5   Than when it was a-doing.
SICINIUS   Bid them home.
    Say their great enemy is gone, and they
7   Stand in their ancient strength.
BRUTUS   Dismiss them home.
                                    [Exit Aedile.]
    Here comes his mother.
SICINIUS   Let's not meet her.
BRUTUS   Why?
SICINIUS
    They say she's mad.
            Enter Volumnia, Virgilia, and Menenius.
BRUTUS
    They have ta'en note of us. Keep on your way.
VOLUMNIA
11 O, y' are well met. The hoarded plague o' th' gods
    Requite your love!
MENENIUS   Peace, peace. Be not so loud.

IV, ii A street in Rome   1 *home* go home   5 *a-doing* being done   7 *ancient*
previous   11 *hoarded* accumulated

VOLUMNIA
    If that I could for weeping, you should hear –
    Nay, and you shall hear some.
        [To Brutus]   Will you be gone?
VIRGILIA [to Sicinius]
    You shall stay too. I would I had the power
    To say so to my husband.
SICINIUS   Are you mankind?   16
VOLUMNIA
    Ay, fool, is that a shame? Note but this fool.
    Was not a man my father? Hadst thou foxship   18
    To banish him that struck more blows for Rome
    Than thou hast spoken words?
SICINIUS   O blessed heavens!
VOLUMNIA
    Moe noble blows than ever thou wise words,   21
    And for Rome's good. I'll tell thee what – Yet go.
    Nay, but thou shalt stay too. I would my son
    Were in Arabia, and thy tribe before him,   24
    His good sword in his hand.
SICINIUS   What then?
VIRGILIA   What then?
    He'ld make an end of thy posterity.
VOLUMNIA
    Bastards and all.
    Good man, the wounds that he does bear for Rome!
MENENIUS
    Come, come, peace.
SICINIUS
    I would he had continued to his country
    As he began, and not unknit himself   31
    The noble knot he made.
BRUTUS   I would he had.

16 *mankind* masculine, human 18 *foxship* animal cunning 21 *Moe* more
24 *Arabia* the desert 31–32 *unknit . . . knot* himself undone the patriotic ties

VOLUMNIA

'I would he had'?'Twas you incensed the rabble.
Cats, that can judge as fitly of his worth
As I can of those mysteries which heaven
Will not have earth to know!

BRUTUS   Pray, let us go.

VOLUMNIA

Now, pray, sir, get you gone.
You have done a brave deed. Ere you go, hear this:
As far as doth the Capitol exceed
The meanest house in Rome, so far my son, –
This lady's husband here, this, do you see? –
Whom you have banished, does exceed you all.

BRUTUS

Well, well, we'll leave you.

SICINIUS   Why stay we to be baited

44   With one that wants her wits?   *Exeunt Tribunes.*

VOLUMNIA   Take my prayers with you.
I would the gods had nothing else to do
But to confirm my curses. Could I meet 'em
But once a day, it would unclog my heart
Of what lies heavy to't.

48 MENENIUS   You have told them home;
And, by my troth, you have cause. You'll sup with me?

VOLUMNIA

Anger's my meat. I sup upon myself,
And so shall starve with feeding. Come, let's go.

52   Leave this faint puling, and lament as I do,
In anger, Juno-like. Come, come, come.

MENENIUS   Fie, fie, fie!
                                          Exeunt.

*

44 *wants* lacks   48 *home* off   52 *puling* whimpering

CORIOLANUS

Enter a Roman and a Volsce. IV, iii

ROMAN I know you well, sir, and you know me. Your name, I think, is Adrian.

VOLSCE It is so, sir. Truly, I have forgot you.

ROMAN I am a Roman; and my services are, as you are, against 'em. Know you me yet?

VOLSCE Nicanor, no?

ROMAN The same, sir.

VOLSCE You had more beard when I last saw you; but your favor is well appeared by your tongue. What's the 9 news in Rome? I have a note from the Volscian state to find you out there. You have well saved me a day's journey.

ROMAN There hath been in Rome strange insurrections: the people against the senators, patricians, and nobles.

VOLSCE Hath been? is it ended then? Our state thinks not so. They are in a most warlike preparation, and hope to come upon them in the heat of their division.

ROMAN The main blaze of it is past, but a small thing would make it flame again; for the nobles receive so to heart the banishment of that worthy Coriolanus that they are in a ripe aptness to take all power from the people and to pluck from them their tribunes for ever. This lies glowing, I can tell you, and is almost mature for the violent breaking out.

VOLSCE Coriolanus banished?

ROMAN Banished, sir.

VOLSCE You will be welcome with this intelligence, Nicanor.

ROMAN The day serves well for them now. I have heard it 28 said, the fittest time to corrupt a man's wife is when she's fall'n out with her husband. Your noble Tullus Aufidius will appear well in these wars, his great opposer, Coriolanus, being now in no request of his country.

VOLSCE He cannot choose. I am most fortunate, thus 33

IV, iii The highway to Antium   9 *favor* face; *appeared* made apparent   28 *them* the Volscians   33 *choose* help appearing well

117

accidentally to encounter you. You have ended my
business, and I will merrily accompany you home.

36 ROMAN I shall, between this and supper, tell you most
strange things from Rome, all tending to the good of
their adversaries. Have you an army ready, say you?

39 VOLSCE A most royal one: the centurions and their
40 charges, distinctly billeted, already in th' entertainment,
and to be on foot at an hour's warning.

ROMAN I am joyful to hear of their readiness, and am the
man, I think, that shall set them in present action. So,
sir, heartily well met, and most glad of your company.

VOLSCE You take my part from me, sir. I have the most
cause to be glad of yours.

ROMAN Well, let us go together.   *Exeunt.*

*

IV, iv   *Enter Coriolanus in mean apparel, disguised and*
muffled.

CORIOLANUS
A goodly city is this Antium. City,
'Tis I that made thy widows. Many an heir
3   Of these fair edifices 'fore my wars
Have I heard groan and drop. Then know me not,
Lest that thy wives with spits and boys with stones
6   In puny battle slay me.
Enter a Citizen.   Save you, sir.

CITIZEN
And you.

CORIOLANUS Direct me, if it be your will,
8   Where great Aufidius lies. Is he in Antium?

CITIZEN
He is, and feasts the nobles of the state

36 *this* now   39 *centurions* officers each commanding a century, i.e. a
hundred men   40 *distinctly* separately; *entertainment* service
IV, iv Before the house of Aufidius in Antium   3 *'fore* before   6 *puny*
petty; *Save* God save   8 *lies* lodges

At his house this night.

CORIOLANUS   Which is his house, beseech you?

CITIZEN
This, here before you.

CORIOLANUS   Thank you, sir. Farewell.

Exit Citizen.

O world, thy slippery turns! Friends now fast sworn,
Whose double bosoms seems to wear one heart,
Whose hours, whose bed, whose meal and exercise
Are still together; who twin, as 'twere, in love   15
Unseparable, shall within this hour,
On a dissension of a doit, break out   ·   17
To bitterest enmity. So, fellest foes,   18
Whose passions and whose plots have broke their sleep
To take the one the other, by some chance,
Some trick not worth an egg, shall grow dear friends   21
And interjoin their issues. So with me.   22
My birthplace hate I, and my love 's upon
This enemy town. I'll enter. If he slay me,
He does fair justice; if he give me way,   25
I'll do his country service.   *Exit.*

*

Music plays. Enter a Servingman.   IV, v

FIRST SERVINGMAN Wine, wine, wine! What service is
here? I think our fellows are asleep.   *[Exit.]* 2

Enter another Servingman.

SECOND SERVINGMAN Where's Cotus? My master calls
for him. Cotus!   *Exit.*

Enter Coriolanus.

CORIOLANUS
A goodly house. The feast smells well, but I
Appear not like a guest.

15 *still* always   17 *dissension . . . doit* trivial dispute   18 *fellest* fiercest   21
trick trifle   22 *interjoin their issues* join fortunes   25 *give me way* grant my
request
IV, v Within the house of Aufidius   2 *fellows* companions

Enter the first Servingman.

FIRST SERVINGMAN What would you have, friend? Whence are you? Here's no place for you. Pray, go to the door.   *Exit.*

CORIOLANUS
I have deserved no better entertainment,
In being Coriolanus.

Enter second Servant.

SECOND SERVINGMAN Whence are you, sir? Has the porter his eyes in his head, that he gives entrance to such companions? Pray, get you out.

CORIOLANUS Away!

SECOND SERVINGMAN Away? get you away!

CORIOLANUS Now th' art troublesome.

SECOND SERVINGMAN Are you so brave? I'll have you
18   talked with anon.

Enter third Servingman ; the first meets him.

THIRD SERVINGMAN What fellow's this?

FIRST SERVINGMAN A strange one as ever I looked on. I cannot get him out o' th' house. Prithee, call my master to him.

THIRD SERVINGMAN What have you to do here, fellow?
23   Pray you, avoid the house.

CORIOLANUS Let me but stand; I will not hurt your hearth.

THIRD SERVINGMAN What are you?

CORIOLANUS A gentleman.

27   THIRD SERVINGMAN A marv'llous poor one.

CORIOLANUS True, so I am.

THIRD SERVINGMAN Pray you, poor gentleman, take up some other station. Here's no place for you. Pray you, avoid. Come.

32   CORIOLANUS Follow your function, go, and batten on cold bits.

Pushes him away from him.

18 *anon* at once   23 *avoid* leave   27 *marv'llous* curiously   32 *batten* grow fat

THIRD SERVINGMAN What, you will not? Prithee, tell
my master what a strange guest he has here.
SECOND SERVINGMAN And I shall.
                                        Exit second Servingman.
THIRD SERVINGMAN Where dwell'st thou?
CORIOLANUS Under the canopy.   38
THIRD SERVINGMAN Under the canopy?
CORIOLANUS Ay.
THIRD SERVINGMAN Where's that?
CORIOLANUS I' th' city of kites and crows.   42
THIRD SERVINGMAN I' th' city of kites and crows?
What an ass it is! Then thou dwell'st with daws too?   44
CORIOLANUS No, I serve not thy master.
THIRD SERVINGMAN How, sir? Do you meddle with
my master?
CORIOLANUS Ay, 'tis an honester service than to meddle
with thy mistress.
Thou prat'st, and prat'st. Serve with thy trencher.   50
Hence!
            Beats him away.
            Enter Aufidius with the [second] Servingman.
AUFIDIUS Where is this fellow?
SECOND SERVINGMAN Here, sir. I'd have beaten him
like a dog, but for disturbing the lords within.
AUFIDIUS
Whence com'st thou? What wouldst thou? Thy name?
Why speak'st not? Speak, man. What's thy name?
CORIOLANUS   If, Tullus,
Not yet thou know'st me, and, seeing me, dost not
Think me for the man I am, necessity   57
Commands me name myself.   58
AUFIDIUS   What is thy name?
CORIOLANUS
A name unmusical to the Volscians' ears,

38 *canopy* sky (metaphorical)   42 *kites and crows* birds of prey   44 *daws*
foolish birds   50 *trencher* plate; *Hence* get away   57 *Think* take   58 *name*
to name

And harsh in sound to thine.

AUFIDIUS   Say, what's thy name?
Thou hast a grim appearance, and thy face
Bears a command in't; though thy tackle's torn,
Thou show'st a noble vessel. What's thy name?

CORIOLANUS
Prepare thy brow to frown. Know'st thou me yet?

AUFIDIUS
I know thee not. Thy name?

CORIOLANUS
My name is Caius Marcius, who hath done
To thee particularly and to all the Volsces
Great hurt and mischief; thereto witness may
69 My surname, Coriolanus. The painful service,
The extreme dangers, and the drops of blood
Shed for my thankless country are requited
72 But with that surname – a good memory,
And witness of the malice and displeasure
Which thou shouldst bear me. Only that name remains.
75 The cruelty and envy of the people,
Permitted by our dastard nobles, who
Have all forsook me, hath devoured the rest;
And suffered me by th' voice of slaves to be
79 Whooped out of Rome. Now this extremity
Hath brought me to thy hearth, not out of hope –
Mistake me not – to save my life; for if
I had feared death, of all the men i' th' world
83 I would have 'voided thee; but in mere spite,
84 To be full quit of those my banishers,
Stand I before thee here. Then if thou hast
86 A heart of wreak in thee, that wilt revenge
Thine own particular wrongs, and stop those maims
Of shame seen through thy country, speed thee straight,
And make my misery serve thy turn. So use it

69 *painful* laborious   72 *memory* memorial   75 *cruelty and envy* envious
cruelty   79 *Whooped* shouted   83 *mere* pure   84 *full quit of* completely
even with   86 *heart of wreak* vengeful heart; *that wilt* so that thou wilt

That my ~~revengeful~~ services may prove
As benefits to thee ; for I will fight
Against my cank'red country with the spleen   92
Of all the under fiends. But if so be   93
Thou dar'st not this, and that to prove more fortunes   94
Th' art tired, then, in a word, I also am
Longer to live most weary ; and present
My throat to thee and to thy ancient malice ;
Which not to cut would show thee but a fool,
Since I have ever followed thee with hate,
Drawn tuns of blood out of thy country's breast,
And cannot live but to thy shame, unless
It be to do thee service.

AUFIDIUS   O Marcius, Marcius !
Each word thou hast spoke hath weeded from my heart
A root of ancient envy. If Jupiter
Should from yond cloud speak divine things,
And say ''Tis true,' I'd not believe them more
Than thee, all-noble Marcius. Let me twine
Mine arms about thy body, whereagainst   108
My grainèd ash an hundred times hath broke,   109
And scarred the moon with splinters. Here I clip   110
The anvil of my sword, and do contest
As hotly and as nobly with thy love
As ever in ambitious strength I did
Contend against thy valor. Know thou first,
I loved the maid I married ; never man
Sighed truer breath. But that I see thee here,
Thou noble thing, more dances my rapt heart   117
Than when I first my wedded mistress saw
Bestride my threshold. Why, thou Mars, I tell thee,   119
We have a power on foot ; and I had purpose
Once more to hew thy target from thy brawn,   121

---

92 *cank'red* corrupted; *spleen* anger   93 *under* infernal   94 *prove* try   108
whereagainst against which   109 *grainèd ash* wooden lance   110 *clip*
embrace   117 *rapt* enraptured   119 *Bestride* step over   121 *target* shield;
brawn muscular arm

122 Or lose mine arm for't. Thou hast beat me out
123 Twelve several times, and I have nightly since
Dreamt of encounters 'twixt thyself and me.
We have been down together in my sleep,
Unbuckling helms, fisting each other's throat,
127 And waked half dead with nothing. Worthy Marcius,
128 Had we no other quarrel else to Rome, but that
Thou art thence banished, **we would** muster all
From twelve to seventy, and, pouring war
Into the bowels of ungrateful Rome,
132 Like a bold flood o'erbeat. O, come, go in,
And take our friendly senators by th' hands,
Who now are here, taking their leaves of me,
Who am prepared against your territories,
Though not for Rome itself.

CORIOLANUS   You bless me, gods!
AUFIDIUS
137 Therefore, most absolute sir, if thou wilt have
The leading of thine own revenges, take
139 Th' one half of my commission; and set down –
As best thou art experienced, since thou know'st
Thy country's strength and weakness – thine own ways,
Whether to knock against the gates of Rome,
Or rudely visit them in parts remote,
144 To fright them ere destroy. But come in.
Let me commend thee first to those that shall
Say yea to thy desires. A thousand welcomes!
And more a friend than e'er an enemy;
Yet, Marcius, that was much. Your hand. Most wel-
come!   *Exeunt.*
        Enter two of the Servingmen.
FIRST SERVINGMAN Here's a strange alteration!

---

122 *out* thoroughly   123 *several* different   127 *waked* I have awakened
128 *to* against   132 *o'erbeat* overflow violently   137 *absolute* perfect   139
commission command; *set down* decide   144 *ere destroy* before destroying
them

SECOND SERVINGMAN By my hand, I had thought to
have strucken him with a cudgel; and yet my mind gave 151
me his clothes made a false report of him.

FIRST SERVINGMAN What an arm he has! He turned
me about with his finger and his thumb as one would set
up a top.

SECOND SERVINGMAN Nay, I knew by his face that
there was something in him. He had, sir, a kind of face,
methought – I cannot tell how to term it.

FIRST SERVINGMAN He had so, looking as it were –
Would I were hanged, but I thought there was more in
him than I could think.

SECOND SERVINGMAN So did I, I'll be sworn. He is
simply the rarest man i' th' world.

FIRST SERVINGMAN I think he is. But a greater soldier
than he you wot on.   164

SECOND SERVINGMAN Who, my master?

FIRST SERVINGMAN Nay, it's no matter for that.   166

SECOND SERVINGMAN Worth six on him.

FIRST SERVINGMAN Nay, not so neither. But I take him
to be the greater soldier.

SECOND SERVINGMAN Faith, look you, one cannot tell
how to say that. For the defense of a town, our general is
excellent.

FIRST SERVINGMAN Ay, and for an assault too.
          Enter the third Servingman.

THIRD SERVINGMAN O slaves, I can tell you news.
News, you rascals!

BOTH [FIRST AND SECOND] What, what, what? Let's
partake.

THIRD SERVINGMAN I would not be a Roman, of all
nations. I had as lief be a condemned man.

BOTH Wherefore? Wherefore?

THIRD SERVINGMAN Why, here's he that was wont to   180
thwack our general, Caius Marcius.

---

151 *gave* suggested to   164 *wot on* know of   166 *it's . . . that* never mind
about names

FIRST SERVINGMAN Why do you say, 'thwack our general'?

THIRD SERVINGMAN I do not say, 'thwack our general,' but he was always good enough for him.

SECOND SERVINGMAN Come, we are fellows and friends. He was ever too hard for him; I have heard him say so himself.

FIRST SERVINGMAN He was too hard for him directly,
189 to say the troth on't. Before Corioles he scotched him
190 and notched him like a carbonado.

191 **SECOND SERVINGMAN** An he had been cannibally given, he might have boiled and eaten him too.

FIRST SERVINGMAN But more of thy news?

194 **THIRD SERVINGMAN** Why, he is so made on here within, as if he were son and heir to Mars; set at upper end o' th'
196 table; no question asked him by any of the senators, but
197 they stand bald before him. Our general himself makes a
198 mistress of him; sanctifies himself with's hand, and turns up the white o' th' eye to his discourse. But the bottom of the news is, our general is cut i' th' middle and but one half of what he was yesterday; for the other has half, by the entreaty and grant of the whole table.
203 He'll go, he says, and sowl the porter of Rome gates by th' ears. He will mow all down before him, and leave
205 his passage polled.

SECOND SERVINGMAN And he's as like to do't as any man I can imagine.

THIRD SERVINGMAN Do't? he will do't! for, look you, sir, he has as many friends as enemies; which friends, sir, as it were, durst not, look you, sir, show themselves,
211 as we term it, his friends whilst he's in directitude.

FIRST SERVINGMAN Directitude? what's that?

---

189 *troth* truth; *scotched* slashed   **190** *carbonado* meat cut for broiling   **191** *An* if   **194** *made on* made much of   **196** *but* unless   **197** *bald* bare-headed   **198** *sanctifies . . . hand* touches his hand as if it were a sacred relic   **203** *sowl* pull roughly   **205** *polled* stripped bare   **211** *directitude* discredit (verbal blunder)

THIRD SERVINGMAN But when they shall see, sir, his
crest up again, and the man in blood, they will out of
their burrows like conies after rain, and revel all with him. 215

FIRST SERVINGMAN But when goes this forward?

THIRD SERVINGMAN To-morrow, to-day, presently. 217
You shall have the drum struck up this afternoon. 'Tis,
as it were, a parcel of their feast, and to be executed ere 219
they wipe their lips.

SECOND SERVINGMAN Why, then we shall have a stir-
ring world again. This peace is nothing but to rust iron,
increase tailors, and breed ballad-makers.

FIRST SERVINGMAN Let me have war, say I. It exceeds
peace as far as day does night. It's sprightly, waking,
audible, and full of vent. Peace is a very apoplexy, 226
lethargy; mulled, deaf, sleepy, insensible; a getter of 227
more bastard children than war 's a destroyer of men.

SECOND SERVINGMAN 'Tis so; and as war, in some sort,
may be said to be a ravisher, so it cannot be denied but
peace is a great maker of cuckolds.

FIRST SERVINGMAN Ay, and it makes men hate one another.

THIRD SERVINGMAN Reason: because they then less
need one another. The wars for my money. I hope to see
Romans as cheap as Volscians. They are rising, they are
rising.

BOTH [FIRST AND SECOND] In, in, in, in!   *Exeunt.*

*

Enter the two Tribunes, Sicinius and Brutus.   IV, vi

SICINIUS
We hear not of him, neither need we fear him;
His remedies are tame: the present peace   2

215 *conies* rabbits   217 *presently* immediately   219 *parcel* part   226 *audible*
capable of hearing; *apoplexy* paralysis   227 *mulled* stupefied; *getter* begetter
IV, vi A public place in Rome   2 *His remedies* the remedies against him;
tame mild

> And quietness of the people, which before
> Were in wild hurry. Here do we make his friends
> Blush that the world goes well, who rather had,
6 Though they themselves did suffer by't, behold
7 Dissentious numbers pest'ring streets than see
> Our tradesmen singing in their shops and going
> About their functions friendly.

BRUTUS

10 We stood to't in good time.
>   *Enter Menenius.*   Is this Menenius?

SICINIUS
> 'Tis he, 'tis he! O, he is grown most kind of late. –
> Hail, sir!

MENENIUS Hail to you both!

SICINIUS   Your Coriolanus
> Is not much missed, but with his friends.
> The commonwealth doth stand, and so would do,
> Were he more angry at it.

MENENIUS
> All's well; and might have been much better, if
17 He could have temporized.

SICINIUS   Where is he, hear you?

MENENIUS
> Nay, I hear nothing. His mother and his wife
> Hear nothing from him.
>   *Enter three or four Citizens.*

ALL
> The gods preserve you both!

20 SICINIUS   Good-e'en, our neighbors.

BRUTUS
> Good-e'en to you all, good-e'en to you all.

FIRST CITIZEN
> Ourselves, our wives, and children, on our knees,
> Are bound to pray for you both.

SICINIUS   Live, and thrive!

---

6 *behold* beheld   7 *pest'ring* crowding   10 *stood to't* took a stand   17 *temporized* compromised   20 *Good-e'en* good evening

BRUTUS
Farewell, kind neighbors. We wished Coriolanus
Had loved you as we did.

CITIZENS   Now the gods keep you!

BOTH TRIBUNES
Farewell, farewell.   *Exeunt Citizens*.

SICINIUS
This is a happier and more comely time   27
Than when these fellows ran about the streets,
Crying confusion.

BRUTUS   Caius Marcius was
A worthy officer i' th' war, but insolent,
O'ercome with pride, ambitious past all thinking,
Self-loving –

SICINIUS   And affecting one sole throne
Without assistance.   33

MENENIUS   I think not so.

SICINIUS
We should by this, to all our lamentation,   34
If he had gone forth consul, found it so.

BRUTUS
The gods have well prevented it, and Rome
Sits safe and still without him.
          Enter an Aedile.

AEDILE   Worthy tribunes,
There is a slave whom we have put in prison
Reports the Volsces with two several powers   39
Are ent'red in the Roman territories,
And with the deepest malice of the war
Destroy what lies before 'em.

MENENIUS   'Tis Aufidius,
Who, hearing of our Marcius' banishment,
Thrusts forth his horns again into the world;
Which were inshelled when Marcius stood for Rome,   45
And durst not once peep out.

27 *comely* decent   33 *assistance* partners   34 *this* this time   39 *several*
separate   45 *inshelled* drawn in; *stood* stood up

SICINIUS   Come, what talk you
Of Marcius?

BRUTUS
Go see this rumorer whipped. It cannot be
The Volsces dare break with us.

MENENIUS   Cannot be!
We have record that very well it can,
And three examples of the like hath been
52   Within my age. But reason with the fellow,
Before you punish him, where he heard this,
54   Lest you shall chance to whip your information
And beat the messenger who bids beware
Of what is to be dreaded.

SICINIUS   Tell not me.
I know this cannot be.

BRUTUS   Not possible.

     Enter a Messenger.

MESSENGER
The nobles in great earnestness are going
All to the Senate House. Some news is coming
60   That turns their countenances.

SICINIUS   'Tis this slave –
61   Go whip him 'fore the people's eyes – his raising,
Nothing but his report.

MESSENGER   Yes, worthy sir.
63   The slave's report is seconded; and more,
64   More fearful, is delivered.

SICINIUS   What more fearful?

MESSENGER
It is spoke freely out of many mouths –
How probable I do not know – that Marcius,
Joined with Aufidius, leads a power 'gainst Rome,
68   And vows revenge as spacious as between

---

52 *reason* discuss   54 *information* source of information   60 *turns* changes
61 *raising* incitement   63 *seconded* confirmed   64 *delivered* reported
68–69 *as spacious . . . thing* embracing all

The young'st and oldest thing.

SICINIUS   This is most likely!

BRUTUS
Raised only, that the weaker sort may wish   70
Good Marcius home again.

SICINIUS   The very trick on't.

MENENIUS
This is unlikely.
He and Aufidius can no more atone   73
Than violent'st contrariety.   74

    Enter [another] Messenger.

MESSENGER
You are sent for to the Senate.
A fearful army, led by Caius Marcius
Associated with Aufidius, rages
Upon our territories; and have already
O'erborne their way, consumed with fire, and took   79
What lay before them.

    Enter Cominius.

COMINIUS   O, you have made good work!

MENENIUS
What news? What news?

COMINIUS
You have holp to ravish your own daughters and   82
To melt the city leads upon your pates,   83
To see your wives dishonored to your noses, –

MENENIUS
What's the news? What's the news?

COMINIUS
Your temples burnèd in their cement, and
Your franchises, whereon you stood, confined   87
Into an auger's bore.   88

---

70 *Raised* set going **73** *atone* be reconciled **74** *violent'st contrariety*
opposite extremes **79** *O'erborne* crushed down **82** *holp* helped **83** *leads*
leaden roofs **87** *franchises* political rights; *whereon you stood* on which you
insisted **88** *auger's bore* smallest aperture

MENENIUS   Pray now, your news ? –
You have made fair work, I fear me. – Pray, your news ? –
If Marcius should be joined with Volscians –
COMINIUS   If ?
He is their god. He leads them like a thing
Made by some other deity than nature,
That shapes man better ; and they follow him
Against us brats with no less confidence
Than boys pursuing summer butterflies
Or butchers killing flies.
MENENIUS   You have made good work,
You and your apron-men ! you that stood so much
98   Upon the voice of occupation and
The breath of garlic-eaters !
COMINIUS   He'll shake
Your Rome about your ears.
MENENIUS   As Hercules
101   Did shake down mellow fruit. You have made fair work !
BRUTUS
But is this true, sir ?
COMINIUS   Ay, and you'll look pale
Before you find it other. All the regions
104   Do smilingly revolt ; and who resists
Are mocked for valiant ignorance,
106   And perish constant fools. Who is't can blame him ?
Your enemies and his find something in him.
MENENIUS
We are all undone, unless
The noble man have mercy.
COMINIUS   Who shall ask it ?
The tribunes cannot do't for shame ; the people
Deserve such pity of him as the wolf
Does of the shepherds. For his best friends, if they
113   Should say, 'Be good to Rome,' they charged him even

98 *voice of occupation* mechanics' suffrage   101 *fruit* apples of Hesperides
104 *who* whoever   106 *constant* loyal   113 *charged* would enjoin

As those should do that had deserved his hate,
And therein showed like enemies.   115
MENENIUS   'Tis true.
If he were putting to my house the brand
That should consume it, I have not the face
To say, 'Beseech you, cease.' You have made fair hands, 118
You and your crafts! You have crafted fair!   119
COMINIUS   You have brought
A trembling upon Rome, such as was never
S' incapable of help.
TRIBUNES   Say not we brought it.
MENENIUS
How? Was 't we? We loved him; but, like beasts
And cowardly nobles, gave way unto your clusters,   123
Who did hoot him out o' th' city.
COMINIUS   But I fear
They'll roar him in again. Tullus Aufidius,
The second name of men, obeys his points   126
As if he were his officer. Desperation
Is all the policy, strength, and defense
That Rome can make against them.
        Enter a troop of Citizens.
MENENIUS   Here come the clusters.
And is Aufidius with him? – You are they
That made the air unwholesome, when you cast
Your stinking greasy caps in hooting at
Coriolanus' exile. Now he's coming;
And not a hair upon a soldier's head
Which will not prove a whip. As many coxcombs   135
As you threw caps up will he tumble down,
And pay you for your voices. 'Tis no matter.
If he could burn us all into one coal,
We have deserved it.

---

115 *showed* would appear   118 *made fair hands* done a fine job (ironic)   119 *crafted fair* intrigued beautifully   123 *clusters* crowds   126 *of* among; *points* directions   135 *coxcombs* fool's caps

OMNES
Faith, we hear fearful news.

140 FIRST CITIZEN   For mine own part,
When I said banish him, I said 'twas pity.

SECOND CITIZEN And so did I.

THIRD CITIZEN And so did I ; and, to say the truth, so
did very many of us. That we did, we did for the best ;
and though we willingly consented to his banishment,
yet it was against our will.

COMINIUS
Y' are goodly things, you voices !

MENENIUS   You have made
148   Good work, you and your cry ! Shall's to the Capitol ?

COMINIUS
O, ay, what else ?   ·   *Exeunt both.*

SICINIUS
Go, masters, get you home ; be not dismayed.
These are a side that would be glad to have
This true, which they so seem to fear. Go home,
And show no sign of fear.

FIRST CITIZEN The gods be good to us ! Come, masters,
let's home. I ever said we were i' th' wrong when we
banished him.

SECOND CITIZEN So did we all. But come, let's home.
                                        Exeunt Citizens.

BRUTUS
I do not like this news.

SICINIUS   Nor I.

BRUTUS
160   Let's to the Capitol. Would half my wealth
Would buy this for a lie !

SICINIUS   Pray, let us go.
                                        Exeunt Tribunes.

                            *

140 *For . . . part* speaking for myself   148 *cry* pack; *Shall's* shall us   160–61
Would . . . lie I would give half my fortune if this were untrue

134

Enter Aufidius, with his Lieutenant. IV, vii

AUFIDIUS
Do they still fly to th' Roman?

LIEUTENANT
I do not know what witchcraft 's in him, but
Your soldiers use him as the grace 'fore meat,
Their talk at table, and their thanks at end;
And you are dark'ned in this action, sir,   5
Even by your own.

AUFIDIUS   I cannot help it now,
Unless by using means I lame the foot   7
Of our design. He bears himself more proudlier,
Even to my person, than I thought he would
When first I did embrace him. Yet his nature
In that's no changeling, and I must excuse   11
What cannot be amended.

LIEUTENANT   Yet I wish, sir, –
I mean for your particular – you had not   13
Joined in commission with him; but either
Had borne the action of yourself, or else
To him had left it solely.

AUFIDIUS
I understand thee well; and be thou sure,
When he shall come to his account, he knows not
What I can urge against him. Although it seems,
And so he thinks, and is no less apparent
To th' vulgar eye, that he bears all things fairly,
And shows good husbandry for the Volscian state,   22
Fights dragon-like, and does achieve as soon   23
As draw his sword: yet he hath left undone
That which shall break his neck or hazard mine,
Whene'er we come to our account.

IV, vii A camp near Rome **5** *dark'ned* eclipsed **7** *means* means whereby
11 *In . . . changeling* is not inconstant in that respect **13** *for your particular*
in your own interests **22** *husbandry* management **23** *achieve* carry out his
intention

LIEUTENANT

27   Sir, I beseech you, think you he'll carry Rome?

AUFIDIUS

28   All places yield to him ere he sits down,
     And the nobility of Rome are his;
     The senators and patricians love him too.
     The tribunes are no soldiers, and their people
     Will be as rash in the repeal as hasty
     To expel him thence. I think he'll be to Rome
34   As is the osprey to the fish, who takes it
35   By sovereignty of nature. First he was
     A noble servant to them, but he could not
37   Carry his honors even. Whether 'twas pride,
38   Which out of daily fortune ever taints
     The happy man; whether defect of judgment,
40   To fail in the disposing of those chances
41   Which he was lord of; or whether nature,
     Not to be other than one thing, not moving
43   From th' casque to th' cushion, but commanding peace
     Even with the same austerity and garb
     As he controlled the war; but one of these,
46   As he hath spices of them all, – not all,
47   For I dare so far free him – made him feared,
     So hated, and so banished. But he has a merit,
49   To choke it in the utt'rance. So our virtues
50   Lie in th' interpretation of the time;
     And power, unto itself most commendable,
52   Hath not a tomb so evident as a chair
     T' extol what it hath done.
     One fire drives out one fire; one nail, one nail;

---

27 *carry* win   **28** *ere . . . down* before he lays siege   **34** *osprey* fish-hawk   **35**
sovereignty predominance   **37** *even* without losing his equilibrium   **38**
daily fortune uninterrupted success; *taints* corrupts   **40** *disposing* making
good use of   **41** *nature* character   **43** *casque* general's helmet; *cushion*
senator's seat   **46** *spices . . . all* a tincture of each   **47** *free* absolve   **49**
To . . . utt'rance enough to suppress the recital of his faults   **50** *the time*
our contemporaries   **52** *not . . . chair* no memorial so certain as a public
rostrum

Rights by rights founder, strengths by strengths do fail.
Come, let's away. When, Caius, Rome is thine,
Thou art poor'st of all ; then shortly art thou mine.   57

Exeunt.

*

Enter *Menenius, Cominius ; Sicinius, Brutus, the*   V, i
two *Tribunes ; with others.*

MENENIUS
No, I'll not go. You hear what he hath said
Which was sometime his general, who loved him   2
In a most dear particular. He called me father.   3
But what o' that ? Go, you that banished him ;
A mile before his tent fall down, and knee   5
The way into his mercy. Nay, if he coyed   6
To hear Cominius speak, I'll keep at home.   7

COMINIUS
He would not seem to know me.   8

MENENIUS   Do you hear ?

COMINIUS
Yet one time he did call me by my name.
I urged our old acquaintance, and the drops
That we have bled together. Coriolanus
He would not answer to ; forbade all names.
He was a kind of nothing, titleless,
Till he had forged himself a name o' th' fire   14
Of burning Rome.

MENENIUS   Why, so. – You have made good work !
A pair of tribunes that have racked for Rome,   16
To make coals cheap ! A noble memory !

COMINIUS
I minded him how royal 'twas to pardon   18

---

57 *shortly* soon
V, i A public place in Rome   2 *Which* who; *sometime* formerly   3 *In . . .*
particular with warmest personal affection   5 *knee* crawl   6 *coyed* dis-
dained   7 *keep* stay   8 *would not seem* pretended not   14 *o'* out of   16
racked striven   18 *minded* reminded

When it was less expected. He replied,
20 It was a bare petition of a state
To one whom they had punished.

MENENIUS   Very well.
Could he say less?

COMINIUS
23 I offered to awaken his regard
For's private friends. His answer to me was,
25 He could not stay to pick them in a pile
Of noisome musty chaff. He said 'twas folly,
For one poor grain or two, to leave unburnt
28 And still to nose th' offense.

MENENIUS   For one poor grain or two?
I am one of those! His mother, wife, his child,
And this brave fellow too, we are the grains;
You are the musty chaff, and you are smelt
Above the moon. We must be burnt for you.

SICINIUS
Nay, pray, be patient. If you refuse your aid
34 In this so-never-needed help, yet do not
Upbraid's with our distress. But, sure, if you
Would be your country's pleader, your good tongue,
More than the instant army we can make,
Might stop our countryman.

MENENIUS   No, I'll not meddle.

SICINIUS
Pray you, go to him.

MENENIUS   What should I do?

BRUTUS
Only make trial what your love can do
For Rome toward Marcius.

MENENIUS   Well, and say that Marcius
42 Return me, as Cominius is returned,
Unheard – what then?

---

20 *bare* mere **23** *offered* attempted **25** *stay . . . them* stop to pick them out
28 *nose* smell; *offense* offensive matter **34** *so-never-needed* never so much
needed **42** *Return* send away

But as a discontented friend, grief-shot   44
   With his unkindness? Say't be so?
SICINIUS   Yet your good will
   Must have that thanks from Rome, after the measure   46
   As you intended well.
MENENIUS   I'll undertake't:
   I think he'll hear me. Yet, to bite his lip
   And hum at good Cominius much unhearts me.   49
   He was not taken well; he had not dined.   50
   The veins unfilled, our blood is cold, and then
   We pout upon the morning, are unapt
   To give or to forgive; but when we have stuffed
   These pipes and these conveyances of our blood   54
   With wine and feeding, we have suppler souls
   Than in our priest-like fasts. Therefore I'll watch him 56
   Till he be dieted to my request,   57
   And then I'll set upon him.
BRUTUS
   You know the very road into his kindness,
   And cannot lose your way.
MENENIUS   Good faith, I'll prove him,
   Speed how it will. I shall ere long have knowledge
   Of my success.   *Exit.* 62
COMINIUS   He'll never hear him.
SICINIUS   Not?
COMINIUS
   I tell you, he does sit in gold, his eye   63
   Red as 'twould burn Rome, and his injury   64
   The jailer to his pity. I kneeled before him.
   'Twas very faintly he said, 'Rise'; dismissed me
   Thus, with his speechless hand. What he would do
   He sent in writing after me; what he would not

---

44 *grief-shot* sorrow-stricken **46-47** *after . . . As* to the extent that **49**
unhearts disheartens **50** *taken well* approached opportunely **54** *convey-*
ances channels **56** *watch* wait for **57** *dieted to* fed to the point of entertain-
ing **62** *success* result **63** *does . . . gold* is enthroned **64** *injury* sense of
injury

69   Bound with an oath to yield to his conditions;
     So that all hope is vain
71   Unless his noble mother and his wife,
     Who, as I hear, mean to solicit him
     For mercy to his country. Therefore let's hence,
74   And with our fair entreaties haste them on.   *Exeunt*.

*

V, ii   *Enter Menenius to the Watch on guard.*

FIRST WATCH
Stay. Whence are you?

SECOND WATCH   Stand, and go back.

MENENIUS
You guard like men; 'tis well. But, by your leave,
I am an officer of state, and come
To speak with Coriolanus.

FIRST WATCH   From whence?

MENENIUS   From Rome.

FIRST WATCH
You may not pass; you must return. Our general
Will no more hear from thence.

SECOND WATCH
You'll see your Rome embraced with fire before
You'll speak with Coriolanus.

8 MENENIUS   Good my friends,
If you have heard your general talk of Rome
10 And of his friends there, it is lots to blanks
    My name hath touched your ears. It is Menenius.

FIRST WATCH
Be't so; go back. The virtue of your name
Is not here passable.

MENENIUS   I tell thee, fellow,

---

69 *Bound* he bound; *to yield* that we should yield   **71** *Unless* except for   **74**
fair courteous
V, ii The Volscian camp before Rome   **8** *Good my friends* my good friends
10 *lots* prizes; *blanks* lottery tickets without value

Thy general is my lover. I have been 14
The book of his good acts, whence men have read
His fame unparalleled, haply amplified; 16
For I have ever verified my friends, 17
Of whom he's chief, with all the size that verity
Would without lapsing suffer. Nay, sometimes,
Like to a bowl upon a subtle ground, 20
I have tumbled past the throw; and in his praise
Have almost stamped the leasing. Therefore, fellow, 22
I must have leave to pass.

FIRST WATCH Faith, sir, if you had told as many lies in
his behalf as you have uttered words in your own, you
should not pass here; no, though it were as virtuous to
lie as to live chastely. Therefore go back. 27

MENENIUS Prithee, fellow, remember my name is
Menenius, always factionary on the party of your 29
general.

SECOND WATCH Howsoever you have been his liar, as
you say you have, I am one that, telling true under him,
must say you cannot pass. Therefore go back.

MENENIUS Has he dined, canst thou tell? For I would
not speak with him till after dinner.

FIRST WATCH You are a Roman, are you?

MENENIUS I am, as thy general is.

FIRST WATCH Then you should hate Rome, as he does.
Can you, when you have pushed out your gates the very 38
defender of them, and in a violent popular ignorance
given your enemy your shield, think to front his re- 40
venges with the easy groans of old women, the virginal
palms of your daughters, or with the palsied intercession
of such a decayed dotant as you seem to be? Can you 43
think to blow out the intended fire your city is ready to

14 *lover* well-wisher   16 *haply* possibly   17 *verified* supported the credit of
20 *bowl* wooden ball; *subtle* deceptive   22 *stamped* attested; *leasing* false-
hood   27 *chastely* honestly   29 *factionary* partisan   38 *out* out of   40
front meet   43 *dotant* dotard

flame in, with such weak breath as this? No, you are
deceived; therefore back to Rome, and prepare for your
execution. You are condemned; our general has sworn
48   you out of reprieve and pardon.

MENENIUS Sirrah, if thy captain knew I were here, he
50   would use me with estimation.

FIRST WATCH Come, my captain knows you not.

MENENIUS I mean thy general.

FIRST WATCH My general cares not for you. Back, I say,
go! lest I let forth your half-pint of blood, – back! –
55   that's the utmost of your having. Back!

MENENIUS Nay, but, fellow, fellow –
    Enter Coriolanus and Aufidius.

CORIOLANUS What's the matter?

MENENIUS Now, you companion, I'll say an errand for
you. You shall know now that I am in estimation; you
60   shall perceive that a Jack guardant cannot office me
61   from my son Coriolanus. Guess but by my entertainment with him. If thou stand'st not i' th' state of hang-
63   ing, or of some death more long in spectatorship and
crueler in suffering, behold now presently, and swound
for what's to come upon thee. *[to Coriolanus]* The
glorious gods sit in hourly synod about thy particular
prosperity, and love thee no worse than thy old father
Menenius does! O my son, my son! Thou art preparing
fire for us. Look thee, here's water to quench it. I was
70   hardly moved to come to thee; but being assured none
but myself could move thee, I have been blown out of
our gates with sighs; and conjure thee to pardon Rome
73   and thy petitionary countrymen. The good gods assuage
thy wrath, and turn the dregs of it upon this varlet here
75   – this, who, like a block, hath denied my access to thee.

---

48 *out of* beyond   50 *use* treat; *estimation* esteem   55 *the ... having* as much
as you have   60 *Jack guardant* knave on guard; *office* officiously keep   61
entertainment reception   63 *spectatorship* watching   70 *hardly* with dif-
ficulty   73 *petitionary* entreating   75 *block* obstruction, blockhead

CORIOLANUS Away!
MENENIUS How? away?
CORIOLANUS
  Wife, mother, child, I know not. My affairs
  Are servanted to others. Though I owe   79
  My revenge properly, my remission lies   80
  In Volscian breasts. That we have been familiar,
  Ingrate forgetfulness shall poison, rather   82
  Than pity note how much. Therefore be gone.
  Mine ears against your suits are stronger than
  Your gates against my force. Yet, for I loved thee,   85
  Take this along. I writ it for thy sake,
      [Gives a letter.]
  And would have sent it. Another word, Menenius,
  I will not hear thee speak. This man, Aufidius,
  Was my beloved in Rome; yet thou behold'st!
AUFIDIUS
  You keep a constant temper.
          Exeunt. Manent the Guard and Menenius.
FIRST WATCH Now, sir, is your name Menenius?
SECOND WATCH 'Tis a spell, you see, of much power.
  You know the way home again.
FIRST WATCH Do you hear how we are shent for keeping 94
  your greatness back?
SECOND WATCH What cause do you think I have to
  swound?
MENENIUS I neither care for th' world nor your general.
  For such things as you, I can scarce think there's any,
  y' are so slight. He that hath a will to die by himself fears 99
  it not from another. Let your general do his worst. For
  you, be that you are, long; and your misery increase 101
  with your age! I say to you, as I was said to, 'Away!'
                                                  Exit.

79 servanted made subservient; owe possess 80 properly as my own;
remission power to pardon 82 Ingrate forgetfulness your ingratitude in
failing to defend me 85 for because 94 shent taken to task 99 by himself
at his own hands 101 long tedious, long-lived

FIRST WATCH A noble fellow, I warrant him.
SECOND WATCH The worthy fellow is our general. He's
the rock, the oak not to be wind-shaken.   *Exit Watch.*

*

V, iii   *Enter Coriolanus and Aufidius [with others].*

CORIOLANUS
We will before the walls of Rome to-morrow
2   Set down our host. My partner in this action,
3   You must report to th' Volscian lords how plainly
I have borne this business.
AUFIDIUS   Only their ends
You have respected; stopped your ears against
The general suit of Rome; never admitted
A private whisper, no, not with such friends
That thought them sure of you.
CORIOLANUS   This last old man,
Whom with a cracked heart I have sent to Rome,
Loved me above the measure of a father;
11 Nay, godded me indeed. Their latest refuge
Was to send him; for whose old love I have –
13 Though I showed sourly to him – once more offered
The first conditions, which they did refuse
15 And cannot now accept. To grace him only,
That thought he could do more, a very little
17 I have yielded to. Fresh embassies and suits,
Nor from the state nor private friends, hereafter
Will I lend ear to.
                Shout within. Ha! What shout is this?
Shall I be tempted to infringe my vow
In the same time 'tis made? I will not.

V, iii Before the tent of Coriolanus 2 *host* army 3 *plainly* straight-
forwardly 11 *godded* idolized; *latest* last 13 *showed* acted 15 *grace*
gratify 17–18 *Fresh . . . friends* neither fresh embassies from the state nor
suits from private friends

Enter Virgilia, Volumnia, Valeria, young Marcius,
with Attendants.

My wife comes foremost; then the honored mould   22
Wherein this trunk was framed, and in her hand   23
The grandchild to her blood. But out, affection!
All bond and privilege of nature, break!
Let it be virtuous to be obstinate.
What is that curt'sy worth? or those doves' eyes,
Which can make gods forsworn? I melt, and am not
Of stronger earth than others. My mother bows,
As if Olympus to a molehill should   30
In supplication nod; and my young boy
Hath an aspect of intercession which
Great nature cries, 'Deny not!' Let the Volsces
Plough Rome and harrow Italy! I'll never
Be such a gosling to obey instinct, but stand
As if a man were author of himself
And knew no other kin.

VIRGILIA   My lord and husband!

CORIOLANUS
These eyes are not the same I wore in Rome.

VIRGILIA
The sorrow that delivers us thus changed   39
Makes you think so.

CORIOLANUS   Like a dull actor now,
I have forgot my part, and I am out,   41
Even to a full disgrace. Best of my flesh,
Forgive my tyranny; but do not say
For that, 'Forgive our Romans.' O, a kiss
Long as my exile, sweet as my revenge!
Now, by the jealous queen of heaven, that kiss   46
I carried from thee dear; and my true lip   47
Hath virgined it e'er since You gods! I prate,   48

---

22 *mould* matrix   23 *trunk* body   30 *Olympus* sacred mountain   39
delivers shows   41 *out* at fault   46 *queen of heaven* Juno   47 *dear* cherished
48 *virgined it* kept it intact

And the most noble mother of the world
Leave unsaluted. Sink, my knee, i' th' earth ;
  Kneels.
Of thy deep duty more impression show
Than that of common sons.

VOLUMNIA   O, stand up blest !
Whilst with no softer cushion than the flint
I kneel before thee, and unproperly
Show duty as mistaken all this while
Between the child and parent.

CORIOLANUS   What is this ?

57 Your knees to me ? to your corrected son ?
58 Then let the pebbles on the hungry beach
59 Fillip the stars ! Then let the mutinous winds
  Strike the proud cedars 'gainst the fiery sun,
61 Murd'ring impossibility, to make
  What cannot be, slight work.

VOLUMNIA   Thou art my warrior ;
63 I holp to frame thee. Do you know this lady ?

CORIOLANUS
64 The noble sister of Publicola,
  The moon of Rome, chaste as the icicle
66 That's curded by the frost from purest snow
67 And hangs on Dian's temple – dear Valeria !

VOLUMNIA
68 This is a poor epitome of yours,
  Which by th' interpretation of full time
70 May show like all yourself.

CORIOLANUS   The god of soldiers,
  With the consent of supreme Jove, inform
  Thy thoughts with nobleness, that thou mayst prove
73 To shame unvulnerable, and stick i' th' wars

---

57 *corrected* chastised 58 *hungry* barren 59 *Fillip* snap with a finger
61 *Murd'ring impossibility* making nothing seem impossible 63 *holp*
helped 64 *Publicola* a famous consul 66 *curded* congealed 67 *Dian*
virgin goddess 68 *epitome* miniature 70 *show* appear 73 *To shame
unvulnerable* incapable of disgrace; *stick* be fixed

Like a great sea-mark, standing every flaw   74
And saving those that eye thee!

VOLUMNIA   Your knee, sirrah.   75

CORIOLANUS
That's my brave boy!

VOLUMNIA
Even he, your wife, this lady, and myself,
Are suitors to you.

CORIOLANUS   I beseech you, peace!
Or, if you'd ask, remember this before:
The thing I have forsworn to grant may never   80
Be held by you denials. Do not bid me
Dismiss my soldiers, or capitulate   82
Again with Rome's mechanics. Tell me not
Wherein I seem unnatural. Desire not
T' allay my rages and revenges with
Your colder reasons.

VOLUMNIA   O, no more, no more!
You have said you will not grant us anything;
For we have nothing else to ask but that
Which you deny already; yet we will ask,
That, if you fail in our request, the blame   90
May hang upon your hardness. Therefore hear us.

CORIOLANUS
Aufidius, and you Volsces, mark; for we'll
Hear naught from Rome in private. – Your request?

VOLUMNIA
Should we be silent and not speak, our raiment
And state of bodies would bewray what life
We have led since thy exile. Think with thyself
How more unfortunate than all living women
Are we come hither; since that thy sight, which should
Make our eyes flow with joy, hearts dance with comforts,
Constrains them weep and shake with fear and sorrow,   100

74 *sea-mark* point serving as guide for navigators; *flaw* gust   75 *sirrah* sir
80 *forsworn* sworn not   82 *capitulate* come to terms   90 *fail in* fail to grant
100 *weep* to weep

147

Making the mother, wife, and child to see
The son, the husband, and the father tearing
103 His country's bowels out. And to poor we
104 Thine enmity 's most capital. Thou barr'st us
Our prayers to the gods, which is a comfort
That all but we enjoy. For how can we,
Alas, how can we for our country pray,
Whereto we are bound, together with thy victory,
109 Whereto we are bound ? Alack, or we must lose
The country, our dear nurse, or else thy person,
Our comfort in the country. We must find
112 An evident calamity, though we had
Our wish which side should win. For either thou
114 Must as a foreign recreant be led
With manacles through our streets, or else
Triumphantly tread on thy country's ruin,
117 And bear the palm for having bravely shed
Thy wife and children's blood. For myself, son,
I purpose not to wait on fortune till
120 These wars determine. If I cannot persuade thee
121 Rather to show a noble grace to both parts
Than seek the end of one, thou shalt no sooner
March to assault thy country than to tread –
Trust to 't, thou shalt not – on thy mother's womb
That brought thee to this world.

VIRGILIA   Ay, and mine,
That brought you forth this boy, to keep your name
Living to time.

127 BOY   A' shall not tread on me !
I'll run away till I am bigger, but then I'll fight.

CORIOLANUS
Not of a woman's tenderness to be
Requires nor child nor woman's face to see.

---

103 *poor we* our poor selves   104 *capital* deadly; *barr'st us* keep us from
109 *or* either   112 *evident* certain   114 *recreant* traitor   117 *palm* emblem
of triumph   120 *determine* end   121 *grace* mercy; *parts* sides   127 *'A* he
(familiar)

I have sat too long.
    [Rises.]
VOLUMNIA   Nay, go not from us thus.
  If it were so that our request did tend
  To save the Romans, thereby to destroy
  The Volsces whom you serve, you might condemn us
  As poisonous of your honor. No, our suit
  Is, that you reconcile them while the Volsces
  May say, 'This mercy we have showed,' the Romans,
  'This we received,' and each in either side
  Give the all-hail to thee and cry, 'Be blest   139
  For making up this peace!' Thou know'st, great son,
  The end of war's uncertain, but this certain,
  That, if thou conquer Rome, the benefit
  Which thou shalt thereby reap is such a name
  Whose repetition will be dogged with curses,
  Whose chronicle thus writ: 'The man was noble   145
  But with his last attempt he wiped it out,   146
  Destroyed his country; and his name remains
  To th' ensuing age abhorred,' Speak to me, son.
  Thou hast affected the fine strains of honor,   149
  To imitate the graces of the gods;
  To tear with thunder the wide cheeks o' th' air,
  And yet to change thy sulphur with a bolt   152
  That should but rive an oak. Why dost not speak?   153
  Think'st thou it honorable for a noble man
  Still to remember wrongs? Daughter, speak you.
  He cares not for your weeping. Speak thou, boy.
  Perhaps thy childishness will move him more
  Than can our reasons. There's no man in the world
  More bound to's mother; yet here he lets me prate
  Like one i' th' stocks. Thou hast never in thy life   160
  Showed thy dear mother any courtesy,   161

---

139 *all-hail* salutation of honor   **145** *writ* will be written   **146** *it* his nobility   **149** *fine strains* refinements   **152** *sulphur* lightning; *with* for; *bolt* thunderbolt   **153** *rive* split   **160** *i' th' stocks* publicly humiliated   **161** *courtesy* special consideration

162   When she, poor hen, fond of no second brood,
     Has clucked thee to the wars, and safely home
     Loaden with honor. Say my request's unjust,
     And spurn me back; but if it be not so,
166   Thou art not honest, and the gods will plague thee
167   That thou restrain'st from me the duty which
     To a mother's part belongs. He turns away.
     Down, ladies! Let us shame him with our knees.
170   To his surname Coriolanus 'longs more pride
     Than pity to our prayers. Down! An end!
     This is the last. So, we will home to Rome,
173   And die among our neighbors. Nay, behold's!
     This boy, that cannot tell what he would have
     But kneels and holds up hands for fellowship,
176   Does reason our petition with more strength
     Than thou hast to deny't. Come, let us go.
178   This fellow had a Volscian to his mother;
     His wife is in Corioles, and this child
     Like him by chance. Yet give us our dispatch.
     I am hushed until our city be afire,
182   And then I'll speak a little.

[Coriolanus] holds her by the hand, silent.

CORIOLANUS   O mother, mother!
183   What have you done? Behold, the heavens do ope,
     The gods look down, and this unnatural scene
     They laugh at. O my mother, mother! O!
     You have won a happy victory to Rome;
     But for your son – believe it, O believe it! –
     Most dangerously you have with him prevailed,
189   If not most mortal to him. But let it come.
     Aufidius, though I cannot make true wars,
191   I'll frame convenient peace. Now, good Aufidius,
     Were you in my stead, would you have heard

162 *When* while; *fond* desirous 166 *honest* just 167 *That* because 170 *'longs* belongs 173 *behold's* behold us 176 *reason* argue for 178 *to* for 182 *a little* i.e. a dying curse 183 *ope* open 189 *mortal* fatally 191 *convenient* appropriate

   A mother less? or granted less, Aufidius?

AUFIDIUS
   I was moved withal.   194

CORIOLANUS   I dare be sworn you were!
   And, sir, it is no little thing to make
   Mine eyes to sweat compassion. But, good sir,
   What peace you'll make, advise me. For my part,
   I'll not to Rome, I'll back with you; and pray you,
   Stand to me in this cause. O mother! wife!   199

AUFIDIUS *[aside]*
   I am glad thou hast set thy mercy and thy honor
   At difference in thee. Out of that I'll work
   Myself a former fortune.   202

CORIOLANUS *[to Volumnia]* Ay, by and by.
   But we will drink together; and you shall bear
   A better witness back than words, which we,   204
   On like conditions, will have counter-sealed.
   Come, enter with us. Ladies, you deserve
   To have a temple built you. All the swords   207
   In Italy, and her confederate arms,   208
   Could not have made this peace.   *Exeunt.*

*

   Enter Menenius and Sicinius.   V, iv

MENENIUS See you yond coign o' th' Capitol, yond   1
   cornerstone?

SICINIUS Why, what of that?

MENENIUS If it be possible for you to displace it with
   your little finger, there is some hope the ladies of Rome,
   especially his mother, may prevail with him. But I say
   there is no hope in't; our throats are sentenced and stay   7
   upon execution.

---

194 *withal* by it 199 *Stand to* support 202 *former fortune* fortune like my
former one 204 *which* i.e. the treaty 207 *a temple* i.e. the Temple of
Women's Fortune 208 *confederate arms* military allies
V, iv A street in Rome 1 *coign* corner 7–8 *stay upon* wait for

SICINIUS Is't possible that so short a time can alter the condition of a man?

11 MENENIUS There is difference between a grub and a butterfly; yet your butterfly was a grub. This Marcius is grown from man to dragon. He has wings; he's more than a creeping thing.

SICINIUS He loved his mother dearly.

MENENIUS So did he me; and he no more remembers his mother now than an eight-year-old horse. The tartness of his face sours ripe grapes. When he walks, he moves
19 like an engine, and the ground shrinks before his tread-
20 ing. He is able to pierce a corslet with his eye; talks like
21 a knell and his hum is a battery. He sits in his state, as a
22 thing made for Alexander. What he bids be done is
23 finished with his bidding. He wants nothing of a god but eternity, and a heaven to throne in.

SICINIUS Yes, mercy, if you report him truly.

26 MENENIUS I paint him in the character. Mark what mercy his mother shall bring from him. There is no more mercy in him than there is milk in a male tiger.
29 That shall our poor city find; and all this is long of you.

SICINIUS The gods be good unto us!

MENENIUS No, in such a case the gods will not be good unto us. When we banished him, we respected not them; and, he returning to break our necks, they respect not us.

Enter a Messenger.

MESSENGER
Sir, if you'd save your life, fly to your house.
The plebeians have got your fellow-tribune,
36 And hale him up and down; all swearing, if
The Roman ladies bring not comfort home,

---

11 *difference* difference   19 *engine* instrument of war   20 *corslet* body-armor   21 *battery* assault; *state* throne   22 *thing . . . Alexander* statue of Alexander the Great   23 *finished . . . bidding* accomplished as soon as ordered; *wants* lacks   26 *in the character* according to his personality   29 *long of* owing to   36 *hale* pull

They'll give him death by inches.
> *Enter another Messenger.*

SICINIUS   What's the news?

MESSENGER
Good news, good news! The ladies have prevailed,
The Volscians are dislodged, and Marcius gone.   40
A merrier day did never yet greet Rome,
No, not th' expulsion of the Tarquins.   42

SICINIUS   Friend,
Art thou certain this is true? is't most certain?

MESSENGER
As certain as I know the sun is fire.
Where have you lurked that you make doubt of it?   45
Ne'er through an arch so hurried the blown tide   46
As the recomforted through th' gates. Why, hark you!   47
> *Trumpets, hautboys; drums beat; all together.*

The trumpets, sackbuts, psalteries, and fifes,   48
Tabors and cymbals and the shouting Romans   49
Make the sun dance. Hark you!
> *A shout within.*

MENENIUS   This is good news.
I will go meet the ladies. This Volumnia
Is worth of consuls, senators, patricians,
A city full; of tribunes, such as you,
A sea and land full. You have prayed well to-day.
This morning for ten thousand of your throats
I'd not have given a doit. Hark, how they joy!   56
> *Sound still, with the shouts.*

SICINIUS
First, the gods bless you for your tidings; next,
Accept my thankfulness.

MESSENGER   Sir, we have all
Great cause to give great thanks.

---

40 *dislodged* retired   **42** *Tarquins* dynasty of tyrants   **45** *lurked* been hiding
46 *blown* swollen   **47** s.d. *hautboys* oboes   **48** *sackbuts* trombones;
psalteries stringed instruments   **49** *Tabors* small drums   **56** *doit* smallest
possible sum

SICINIUS   They are near the city?
MESSENGER
60   Almost at point to enter.
SICINIUS   We will meet them,
       And help the joy.   *Exeunt.*
V, v   *Enter two Senators with Ladies [Volumnia, Virgilia,*
                Valeria] passing over the stage, with other Lords.
SENATOR
       Behold our patroness, the life of Rome!
       Call all your tribes together, praise the gods,
       And make triumphant fires; strew flowers before them.
       Unshout the noise that banished Marcius;
5   Repeal him with the welcome of his mother.
       Cry, 'Welcome, ladies, welcome!'
ALL   Welcome, ladies,
       Welcome!
                 A flourish with drums and trumpets. [Exeunt.]

*

V, vi   *Enter Tullus Aufidius, with Attendants.*
AUFIDIUS
       Go tell the lords o' th' city I am here.
2   Deliver them this paper. Having read it,
       Bid them repair to th' market-place, where I,
4   Even in theirs and in the commons' ears,
5   Will vouch the truth of it. Him I accuse
       The city ports by this hath entered and
       Intends t' appear before the people, hoping
       To purge himself with words. Dispatch.
                        [Exeunt Attendants.]
                 Enter three or four Conspirators of Aufidius' faction.
                                        Most welcome!

60 *at . . . enter* on the point of entering
V, v   5 *Repeal him* recall him from exile
V, vi A public place in Corioli   2 *them* to them   4 *theirs* their ears   5
Him he whom

FIRST CONSPIRATOR
How is it with our general?

AUFIDIUS   Even so
As with a man by his own alms empoisoned
And with his charity slain.

SECOND CONSPIRATOR   Most noble sir,
If you do hold the same intent wherein
You wished us parties, we'll deliver you   13
Of your great danger.

AUFIDIUS   Sir, I cannot tell.
We must proceed as we do find the people.

THIRD CONSPIRATOR
The people will remain uncertain whilst
'Twixt you there's difference; but the fall of either
Makes the survivor heir of all.

AUFIDIUS   I know it;
And my pretext to strike at him admits
A good construction. I raised him, and I pawned   20
Mine honor for his truth; who being so heightened,   21
He watered his new plants with dews of flattery,
Seducing so my friends; and to this end
He bowed his nature, never known before
But to be rough, unswayable, and free.

THIRD CONSPIRATOR
Sir, his stoutness   26
When he did stand for consul, which he lost
By lack of stooping –

AUFIDIUS   That I would have spoke of.
Being banished for't, he came unto my hearth;
Presented to my knife his throat. I took him;
Made him joint-servant with me; gave him way   31
In all his own desires; nay, let him choose
Out of my files, his projects to accomplish,   33
My best and freshest men; served his designments   34

---

13 *parties* to be allies   20 *construction* interpretation   21 *truth* loyalty;
heightened exalted   26 *stoutness* obstinacy   31 *joint-servant* colleague;
gave him way gave way to him   33 *files* ranks   34 *designments* enterprises

35 In mine own person ; holp to reap the fame
36 Which he did end all his ; and took some pride
     To do myself this wrong ; till at the last
     I seemed his follower, not partner, and
39 He waged me with his countenance as if
     I had been mercenary.

FIRST CONSPIRATOR   So he did, my lord.
     The army marvelled at it ; and in the last,
     When he had carried Rome and that we looked
     For no less spoil than glory –

43 AUFIDIUS   There was it !
44 For which my sinews shall be stretched upon him.
45 At a few drops of women's rheum, which are
46 As cheap as lies, he sold the blood and labor
     Of our great action ; therefore shall he die,
48 And I'll renew me in his fall. But, hark !
     *Drums and trumpets sound, with great shouts of the
     People.*

FIRST CONSPIRATOR
49 Your native town you entered like a post,
     And had no welcomes home ; but he returns,
     Splitting the air with noise.

SECOND CONSPIRATOR   And patient fools,
     Whose children he hath slain, their base throats tear
     With giving him glory.

53 THIRD CONSPIRATOR   Therefore, at your vantage,
     Ere he express himself or move the people
     With what he would say, let him feel your sword,
56 Which we will second. When he lies along,
57 After your way his tale pronounced shall bury
58 His reasons with his body.

---

35 *holp* help   36 *end* gather in as a harvest   39 *waged* remunerated;
countenance patronage   43 *There* that   44 *sinews . . . upon* strength shall be
exerted against   45 *rheum* tears   46 *blood and labor* bloody labor   48 *renew
me* be restored   49 *post* messenger   53 *at your vantage* seizing your
opportunity   56 *along* prone   57 *After*   *pronounced* your own version of
the affair   58 *reasons* justification

AUFIDIUS   Say no more.
Here come the lords.
Enter the Lords of the city.

ALL LORDS
You are most welcome home.

AUFIDIUS   I have not deserved it.
But, worthy lords, have you with heed perused
What I have written to you?

ALL   We have.

FIRST LORD   And grieve to hear't.   63
What faults he made before the last, I think   64
Might have found easy fines; but there to end
Where he was to begin, and give away   66
The benefit of our levies, answering us   67
With our own charge, making a treaty where
There was a yielding – this admits no excuse.

AUFIDIUS
He approaches. You shall hear him.
*Enter Coriolanus, marching with Drum and Colors,
the Commoners being with him.*

CORIOLANUS
Hail, lords! I am returned your soldier;
No more infected with my country's love
That when I parted hence, but still subsisting
Under your great command. You are to know   74
That prosperously I have attempted, and   75
With bloody passage led your wars even to   76
The gates of Rome. Our spoils we have brought home   77
Do more than counterpoise a full third part
The charges of the action. We have made peace
With no less honor to the Antiates
Than shame to th' Romans; and we here deliver,
Subscribed by th' consuls and patricians,

---

63 *made* committed 64 *fines* punishments 66 *levies* forces raised;
answering repaying 67 *charge* expenses 74 *prosperously . . . attempted* my
endeavors have been fortunate 75 *passage* course 76 *spoils* plunder which
77 *Do . . . counterpoise* outweigh

Together with the seal o' th' Senate, what
83 We have compounded on.

AUFIDIUS   Read it not, noble lords;
But tell the traitor in the highest degree
He hath abused your powers.

CORIOLANUS
Traitor? how now?

AUFIDIUS   Ay, traitor, Marcius!

CORIOLANUS   Marcius?

AUFIDIUS
Ay, Marcius, Caius Marcius! Dost thou think
I'll grace thee with that robbery, thy stol'n name
Coriolanus in Corioles?
You lords and heads o' th' state, perfidiously
He has betrayed your business and given up,
For certain drops of salt, your city Rome –
I say 'your city' – to his wife and mother;
Breaking his oath and resolution like
A twist of rotten silk; never admitting
Counsel o' th' war; but at his nurse's tears
He whined and roared away your victory,
98 That pages blushed at him and men of heart
Looked wond'ring each at other.

CORIOLANUS   Hear'st thou, Mars?

AUFIDIUS
Name not the god, thou boy of tears!

CORIOLANUS   Ha!

AUFIDIUS   No more.

CORIOLANUS
Measureless liar, thou hast made my heart
102 Too great for what contains it. Boy? O slave!
Pardon me, lords, 'tis the first time that ever
I was forced to scold. Your judgments, my grave lords,
105 Must give this cur the lie; and his own notion –

---

83 *compounded* reached an agreement   98 *That* so that; *heart* courage   102
Too . . . it too swollen for my breast   105 *notion* understanding

Who wears my stripes impressed upon him, that
Must bear my beating to his grave – shall join
To thrust the lie unto him.

FIRST LORD

Peace, both, and hear me speak.

CORIOLANUS

Cut me to pieces, Volsces. Men and lads,
Stain all your edges on me. Boy? False hound!   111
If you have writ your annals true, 'tis there   112
That, like an eagle in a dovecote, I
Fluttered your Volscians in Corioles.
Alone I did it. Boy?

AUFIDIUS   Why, noble lords,
Will you be put in mind of his blind fortune,   116
Which was your shame, by this unholy braggart,
'Fore your own eyes and ears?

ALL CONSPIRATORS   Let him die for't.

ALL PEOPLE Tear him to pieces! – Do it presently! –   119
He killed my son! – My daughter! – He killed my
cousin Marcus! He killed my father!

SECOND LORD

Peace, ho! No outrage. Peace!
The man is noble and his fame folds in   123
This orb o' th' earth. His last offenses to us
Shall have judicious hearing. Stand, Aufidius,   125
And trouble not the peace.

CORIOLANUS   O that I had him,
With six Aufidiuses, or more, his tribe,
To use my lawful sword!

AUFIDIUS   Insolent villain!

ALL CONSPIRATORS

Kill, kill, kill, kill, kill him!

    Draw the Conspirators, and kill Marcius, who falls.
    Aufidius stands on him.

---

111 *edges* swords   112 *there* recorded there   116 *blind fortune* mere luck
119 *presently* at once   123 *folds in* enfolds   125 *judicious* judicial

LORDS   Hold, hold, hold, hold!

AUFIDIUS
  My noble masters, hear me speak.

FIRST LORD   O Tullus –

SECOND LORD
  Thou hast done a deed whereat valor will weep.

THIRD LORD
  Tread not upon him. Masters all, be quiet!
  Put up your swords.

AUFIDIUS
  My lords, when you shall know – as in this rage
  Provoked by him you cannot – the great danger
136 Which this man's life did owe you, you'll rejoice
137 That he is thus cut off. Please it your honors
  To call me to your Senate. I'll deliver
  Myself your loyal servant, or endure
  Your heaviest censure.

FIRST LORD   Bear from hence his body,
  And mourn you for him. Let him be regarded
142 As the most noble corse that ever herald
  Did follow to his urn.

SECOND LORD   His own impatience
  Takes from Aufidius a great part of blame.
  Let's make the best of it.

AUFIDIUS   My rage is gone,
  And I am struck with sorrow. Take him up.
  Help, three o' th' chiefest soldiers; I'll be one.
  Beat thou the drum, that it speak mournfully.
  Trail your steel pikes. Though in this city he
150 Hath widowed and unchilded many a one,
  Which to this hour bewail the injury,
152 Yet he shall have a noble memory.
  Assist.   *Exeunt, bearing the body of Coriolanus.*
                               A dead march sounded.

---

136 *did owe you* possessed for you   137 *Please it* may it please   142 *corse*
corpse   150 *unchilded* deprived of children   152 *memory* memorial